Scordril

Kelsey Drake

Scordril

Matador
9 De Montfort Mews
Leicester LE1 7FW, UK
Tel: (+44) 116 255 9311 / 9312
Email: books@troubador.co.uk
Web: www.troubador.co.uk/matador

Kelsey Drake is Sue Brownless and Eleanor Patrick

ISBN 978 1906510 817

A Cataloguing-in-Publication (CIP) catalogue record for this book is available
from the British Library.

Typeset in 11pt Stempel Garamond by Troubador Publishing Ltd, Leicester, UK
Printed in the UK by The Cromwell Press Ltd, Trowbridge, Wilts, UK

Matador is an imprint of Troubador Publishing Ltd

Dedicated to dragons and dragonfriends everywhere

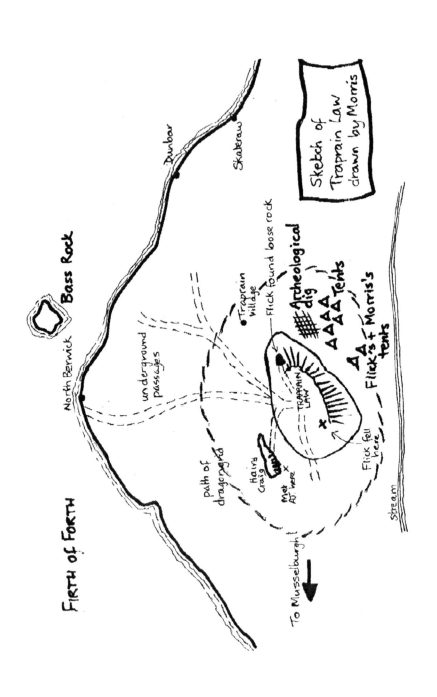

Firth of Forth

Bass Rock

North Berwick

Dunbar

Skateraw

Sketch of
Traprain Law
drawn by Morris

underground
passages

Path of
dragorguild

Hairs
Craig

Met
At here ×

Traprain
village

Flick found loose rock

Archeological
dig

Tents

Flick's + Morris's
tents

TRAPRAIN
LAW

Flick fell
here

To Musselburgh

Stream

CONTENTS

CHAPTER 1

The Messenger – July 1950

Scordril tilted his bronze dragon face upwards and stared uneasily at the birds scattering in the distance. His scales sparkled in the warm morning sun as he stretched his wings backwards, flexing the shoulder muscles. Always vigilant, his sharp dragonmage senses were now on maximum alert.

He was standing watch outside the entrance to the Musselburgh layr. He hadn't anticipated trouble, of course. Few overgrounders, or 'people' as they called themselves in their own tongue, came by here. It was too far away from overgrounder buildings and not near enough the river Esk to be on the way to anywhere special. But that gave him no comfort as he watched a tiny silhouette in the clear sky. Something was heading his way – and overgrounders didn't fly.

Scordril breathed quickly and narrowed his eyes. The unwelcome shape grew in size and familiarity, only to dip suddenly out of sight below some treetops.

Surely he was wrong? Scordril lashed his tail with irritation, disturbing a bee, which began angrily buzzing about his face. No, he hoped he was wrong but it had looked just like a…

Snorting tiny flames into the air at the persistent insect, he tossed his head – and only spotted the shape reappearing from the trees when it was almost too late.

Dragonclaws! thought Scordril, as a surge of fury rushed through his veins. His golden-green eyes glowed brighter as he watched the outline of a young dragon careering towards him. He knew that no dragon would ever fly without a dragonmagic cloud to hide himself unless something was terribly wrong. Instinctively, Scordril drew on his magepower to shield the faltering shape from the view of any overgrounders.

At that moment, the single word »*Help!*« echoed inside Scordril's head.

Wheeling in the sky, like an out-of-control kite, the dragon abruptly plummeted down to earth, landing heavily and tumbling head over tail on the ground with a shrill squeal. The cloud Scordril had called forth disappeared in a puff as he crashed through the coarse grass to the crumpled dragon and skidded to a halt, intent on giving it a piece of his mind before he fetched any help.

»*What leather-brained foolishness…*« he began, but stopped mid-mindspeech and sniffed uncertainly. The young dragon's grey-green form lay huddled and shivering as it clutched a bloodstained wing. It barely raised its head as Scordil bent forward slightly. The dragon was a young male, a stranger to Scordril, terrified, and with the scent of strange magic and danger.

Scordril's temper evaporated. He crouched warily

beside the stricken dragon and spoke more gently. *»I am Scordril, dragonmage of Musselburgh. You are... not known to me, youngone.»* He spoke only with his mind and waited. The injured dragon seemed to rally and tried to sit up.

»Gylning...from Traprain Law.» The dragon sounded proud, then immediately grew agitated. *»Help, please... You must help us.»* Pale green eyes, flecked with silvery lights of anguish, gazed up at Scordril.

»WHAT? Traprain Law?» Astounded, Scordril straightened up, shaking his head. *»But there has been no communication with the dragons there for over a century... One hundred sun-rounds!»* Scordril's rumbling voice wavered in pitch as he struggled to put words to the preposterous idea. *»Nothing since soon after the Great Split when dragons came here to found the Musselburgh layr... This, this is a prank!»* He felt his temper rise again.

»It's true!» Gylning sounded desperate. *»They are trapped... They'll die...»* A fit of shivering briefly seemed to distract the young dragon. But instead of speaking, he'd already sent his experiences of the Traprain layr over the mindlink and Scordril's magesight could sense the recent events through the young dragon's eyes.

What he 'saw' made him gasp. What Gylning had said was true. He sensed doors to a layr that remained closed to dragonbreath, to seldom-used dragonspell words, to sharp dragonclaws digging at the edges before even the sign of a door vanished. He looked down at Gylning's claws; they were indeed worn and bleeding.

Scordril imagined all the dragons trapped inside. He shuddered, reached down, and placed his claws on Gylning's head. The youngone never flinched. »*I… we will help. I will summon the layr council. Come, messenger from Traprain, we will go below.*»

But Scordril knew he'd find it hard to help the stricken Gylning to climb down into the layr. Over time, the dragons had become used to entering the layr via an entrance to the old Victorian sewers, which ran past the closest buildings of Musselburgh and on down to the river and the sea. The dragons' fiery breath had cut an extension from here through the rock, to join up with the buried mine workings that had been their home till then. It was an area long derelict, full of rubble and overgrown. On rare occasions, overgrounders had come to check the old sewers, speaking aloud of renewing them and building shops and offices on the land, oblivious to the fact that dragons used them as a ready-made entrance and exit to a layr buried deep amongst them. But the rickety iron ladder was always difficult. Much more difficult than the original main door, which was hidden like the entrance to a rabbit burrow above the layr. To fit through this iron manhole they had to make themselves smaller, and although Scordril was strong, he was not strong enough to carry an injured dragon and climb the ladder at the same time. He couldn't manage Gylning without hurting him.

So he summoned Brygnon, a sturdy male dragon, who easily carried Gylning down into the main sewer tunnel running towards the layr. Brygnon then returned overground to stand watch instead of Scordril.

Gylning was now able to walk by himself, but visibly recoiled and stumbled when the full summer stench of the sewers reached him. He uttered no sound while Scordril guided him along a ledge beside the slow-running effluent.

»The smell is strong, like a century of sheep sweat, but thankfully does not taint our layr,» said Scordil, grimacing as he pointed to the water flowing sluggishly along the brick tunnel. *»Reach out to steady yourself,»* he added, and showed Gylning how to brush his clawed hands gently along the damp and decaying bricks. Mindful that dragons could normally see well in the dark, Scordril still drew on his magepower to shed a magical golden glow around himself, to make Gylning feel more comfortable. He turned around to check on the youngone every few metres, but Gylning no longer seemed aware of his surroundings as he followed. Scordril guessed that he was fighting the pain in his wing, and admired the youngone's bravery.

Soon, Scordil took a left turn up a separate short tunnel and stopped at the entrance to the layr. He swiftly blew tiny flames on the dark tunnel wall, which glowed orange in response and revealed the pattern of a door. Another breath sparkling with gold lights…and a lock, decorated with ancient runes and drawings of dragons, appeared on one side of the door. A third and final breath shimmering with silver…and the latch opened with a pop.

Silently the door swung inwards, away from the dragons, and Gylning, his pale green eyes flecked with anxious red lights, staggered through behind Scordril. The door creaked shut.

Scordril wasted no time. He sent an urgent bugling-call to summon the council members, and its deep musical tone was still reverberating around the Great Chamber as the dragons started to assemble. He supported Gylning down a short flight of steps into the giant oval hall carved out of the rock by dragonfire, and drew the youngone into the centre of the space. Settling him on a raised ledge before a fire that burned in a shallow pit, Scordril greeted the others in turn and introduced them to Gylning.

First of the mages to stride in was squat and muscular Fenror, with shining purple-grey scales and darting, watchful grey-green eyes. His wings flapped noisily as he moved.

Then came Ygdrann, as tall as Scordril but darker bronze. His piercing brown eyes stared hard at the younger mage, then switched to Gylning.

Next came Kvayn, the female dragonmaster. She was the oldest of the dragon mages and, like Ygdrann and Fenror, had been a hatchling at Traprain Law – though the name was never mentioned these days. But, as Scordril knew, she had been one of the dragons who set up the Musselburgh layr. In fact, her son, Androtta – the last dragon to enter the hall, and introduced by Scordril as the Recorder – had been the first hatchling to be born at Musselburgh. Androtta was responsible for listening and remembering events and then carefully making the entries that would form the layr's Chronicle. He bowed so low his snout almost touched the ground.

Other dragons appeared briefly, bringing clean water in a horn cup for Gylning to drink from, a cloth soaked in soothing ointment for his wounds, and wood for the dwindling fire. Gylning drank deeply, then sat hunched exactly where Scordril had left him in the centre of the room, with the firelight reflecting on his grey-green scales. He held the wad of cloth to his damaged wing hanging loosely at his side. His claws trembled and Scordril, sensing his fear and weakness, moved to sit with the other mages and asked Kvayn, as dragonmaster, to open the meeting.

Scordril remained silent at first and sent strength to Gylning as the other mages began to question the youngone, demanding answers to their suspicions about why a mysterious dragon would appear, literally out of the blue, and expect help. Especially after the Great Split had so effectively separated dragonkin.

»*Why have we not met a dragon from Traprain? Even accidentally we should have met in the skies,*« said Fenror. He banged his claws on his thighs and leaned forward.

Gylning looked confused and shook his head. Kvayn answered for him. »*We fly north and south when we hunt. Why should they? It would be a longer route for them, to the farthest fields or the sea. Besides, traditionally they always flew east or south-east, if my memory hasn't failed me. And it seldom does! I'm not that old!*«

Fenror raised an arm and pointed to Gylning. »*Let him answer!*«

But Ygdrann turned to Fenror. »*No. Kvayn is*

correct, Fenror. *You will not understand, as you were far too young when your father brought you to Musselburgh.*» He turned back to look at Kvayn. »*Do you not recall how we were sent out to scavenge for the elders? All that time ago?*»

Scordril watched Kvayn closely as she nodded. She was obviously sensing that Gylning, depite his fear, tiredness and injuries, was growing frustrated. Scordril, too, was anxious to turn the discussion to the meeting's real purpose. Kvayn took the initiative.

»*Enough! There is time for this later. Now we must hear of the plight that sent Gylning to find us after all this time. Speak, youngone. Tell us your tale so that we can judge it.*»

The Musselburgh mages fell silent and listened to Gylning and his story of the dragons trapped at Traprain Law. And Scordril realised that the scent lingering on Gylning wasn't simply his fear of a stranger.

»*There have been problems for some time,*» said Gylning, straightening up. His gaze shifted among the dragonmages ranged on their sitting ledge around the hall. The torches burning in their wall sconces, and the fire's revitalised flames, cast a dancing light on his earnest face. »*A weakening of our powers, even the magepower, as a strange barrier grew around us. Round the Law… I mean the hill, itself. Becoming stronger and stronger, others said, like a barrier. Still, we came and went. Always finding a way in. Then, as the sun rose early, I… I went out scavenging. I came back later than I should… and when I returned to the layr alone, I* could find no way in! I tried and tried but nothing worked…» Gylning's voice rose and he looked around, as if uncertain whether the mages understood.

»*Nothing?*» Fenror sounded sceptical.

»*Nothing! The door appeared in the rock, yes, but no lock opened to my dragonbreath. Or to any dragonspell words I know. I even tried to open it with force.*» Gylning raised one set of worn claws to show them. »*Then, even the pattern of the door vanished. And my… my breath ceased to burn…*»

The other dragons murmured uneasily before Kvayn spoke.

»*So, no way in, and no fire to use to get out… The others were all trapped, you say. Are you sure?*»

»*Yes. All trapped. And we are many under the Law. I think we have been going out less often since the problems began. I do not know for sure…*» Gylning certainly sounded like he was guessing. »*Ever since the tunnel to the sea became unusable, maybe…*»

»*And no watchdragon!*» Fenror roared.

»*No. Njortin, a mage and our dragonmaster, said not to take turns standing watch. He said he feared it would bring danger and we should stay below whenever possible.*»

»*What danger?*» Kvayn's eyes glittered in the flickering light as she spoke.

»*I… I do not know… Yorheim, my layring teacher, said he asked the magecouncil and got no answer, or none he would tell me. I – er – overheard him, arguing with another of our kin, Jarl, about it.*»

»*Jarl?*» Kvayn hissed quietly. »*Jarl of Traprain.*»

And she flicked her tail, smacking it against the floor. Gylning jumped. Even Androtta, the Recorder, looked startled. Ygdrann glanced uneasily sideways at Kvayn.

Scordril sensed something was wrong although he didn't know what. But he was more concerned with the present than the past, unless the past was relevant. It was time to speak up. He wanted to be sure that the feelings he'd sensed earlier were true and not just imagined. Changing the subject, he turned to Gylning.

»*But you could hear and sense the Traprain Law dragons inside? You knew to come here?*»

»*Yes, of course!*« Ygdrann interrupted, leaning towards the young messenger. »*That's how you knew where we were. Njortin would remember! There was some communication for a few years, I remember.*»

Gylning nodded. »*Yes, it was Njortin. He's very old, the wisest of the dragons at the Law. He tried to send the location of the layr to me. But…but I only understood part of it… I had to fly many dragonspans to get here, without even a dragoncloud to protect me. I couldn't draw on their power. And even when I got close, it was a long time before I recognised the church spire high above the river course. I flew up and down the river. Then I sensed dragonkin…*»

Gylning slumped forward as if utterly exhausted by his explanation. Scordril knew it was time to end the meeting. He stood and raised his chocolate-veined wings.

»*I, for one, believe what I have heard. Surely, we must consider our course of action.*»

Kvayn nodded in response. Her grey face, much

darker than normal, looked thoughtful. *»Let Gylning leave while we speak.»*

The dragonmages shifted on their ledge. Scordril turned to summon help for the youngone. But there was no need.

»I will take the messenger, Gylning...» A female dragon had appeared from the shadows at the rear of the Hall almost as soon as the thought formed.

Scordril recognised Threah, a dragon close to him in years, and wondered if she had been eavesdropping. He knew that news of the strange dragon from Traprain would spread quickly. Threah headed purposefully towards Gylning, her pale blue-grey form moving quietly, reflecting the firelight as she bent to comfort him. Scordril noticed that she carefully took Gylning's arms and steadied him as he stood up. She looked round at the mages before fixing her golden eyes on Scordril.

»It is time for healing, not talk!»

Scordril sensed the amusement of the other mages at Threah's tone. But he also knew that Threah wasn't being rude and kept his irritation in check. He didn't let his gaze waver as he watched Threah lead the youngone to an arched tunnel entrance at the rear of the Hall. He would have his wounds bathed and dressed at Threah's capable claws. Her skill with healing herbs was legendary in the layr.

——⟡⟡⟡——

Gylning was soon settled on his right side on a long flat

stone, a dragon lying-stone. His head rested on a rolled sheepskin. He closed his eyes. Threah cast her own eyes over his thin body, now covered in bruises and scrapes. Most urgent was his wing. The rest would heal with time, but with a badly healed wing, a dragon would be unable to fly. She didn't really want to disturb him as he looked so peaceful, but she needed to examine his wing. As she stretched the wing out, Gylning winced and opened his eyes.

»*I think I broke something as I fell. It sounded that way.*» Gylning's pale green eyes looked up at Threah and then down to his left wing. »*Ow!*»

Threah released the wing gently. »*You're right... The phalange bone just there and perhaps another there...where the skin is torn. And perhaps you have torn the deltoid muscle over your shoulder too. I will call another dragon to assist. Ennasif is not much older than you are, and she's excellent at helping. Just rest while I mindspeak her.*»

While she was waiting for Ennasif, Threah gently bathed Gylning's claws and rubbed a little of her own recipe ointment onto them. It had the scent of summer marigolds and sticky honey.

»*Here I am, Threah. How can I help?*» Ennasif gazed at the stranger on the lying-stone. His eyes were closed again, but Threah saw that they flicked open to look at Ennasif.

»*Ennasif, this is Gylning, from Traprain. He has broken wing bones. I'd like you to help me bind them for healing, please.*» Threah pointed to the pile of sturdy twigs, strips of leather and fleecy wadding all ready at the foot of the lying-stone. »*Let's get started and then you can help with herbs to ease his discomfort.*»

Threah knew it would take a while. She smiled to herself. At least then Gylning could sleep, and after that she was sure he'd have to answer questions all over again, from the curious Ennasif.

———◦/◦/◦———

In the Great Chamber the mages were still hotly discussing Gylning's report. They became more and more animated, and by his frown, poor Androtta looked like he was finding it harder and harder to record the meeting. Scordril raised his eyes to the high ceiling at yet another outburst. Ygdrann was speaking.

»*I remember how it was before the Great Split, even though I was young, barely past 50 sun-rounds.*» His dark eyes blazed with red flecks of concern. »*Yet I don't think it's a plot by the remainder of our kin to destroy us. Why not just come as overgrounders?*»

»*Because no mature dragon can stay morphed as an overgrounder for that length of time! I say why not come as dragons?*» said Fenror, his skin underscoring his sarcasm by its deeper purple flush.

»*Enough! We are mages; behave as a mage!*» Kvayn tossed her head. »*I was older. Not old enough perhaps, but I was there in the midst. Did I not protect the Chronicles themselves? I can remember conflict. It should not be spoken of lightly. As for the Great Split, I recall confusion and half-truths. Elders whispering, 'Jarl* the traitor, Jarl the foolish,' behind our backs. Warning us to have our wits about us without saying why. Nevertheless, I remember strange events, when dragonspells seemed to fail. Events that Gylning's tale brought back to mind. And I say we need to know the facts before we decide. We must look back at the Chronicles for a clue. This is strong magic and the root has to be found and destroyed.»

»We cannot all read the Chronicles! Surely it is the Recorder's task!» Fenror looked as indignant as he sounded.

Scordril felt his anger growing and the argumentative mindspeech was giving him headpain. He rose and began to pace. »Of course we cannot! And the Recorder is just that, the one who records. It is for a mage to read the Chronicles. Only a mage can recall and discuss it in council. I was not at Traprain Law. I will not be biased in my reading. I suggest that I read the Chronicles tonight. I will work all through the night if necessary and return to the council tomorrow. Then we will know more about Traprain, the Great Split and the possible causes of this...this disaster.»

Kvayn spoke next. »Good, very good. Let us hope that you find the answer we seek. I am sure it is there to be found. The Chronicles were once kept by Fargelmir. A good friend, long dead, and an honest and thorough Recorder. It is sad that Garekk, the first Recorder here, died before she had time to pass on her wisdom to Androtta. Still, she was as busy with the founding of Musselburgh as the rest of us. I doubt she spent any time dwelling on the past.»

Kvayn raised her grey wings as she stood up to signal the meeting was over. »*If there is magic working against dragons, we must know. We may have to choose between saving Traprain and protecting ourselves.*»

The other dragons filed out, their tails and wings making leathery sounds against the rock. And then silence descended on the Great Chamber. For once, Scordril felt uncomfortably alone. He shivered despite the fire. *Now is not the time to be afraid*, he told himself resolutely and headed off to collect the Chronicles.

——◦◦◦——

Vanurl, the dragon who was Androtta's aide, accompanied Scordril to the small room where the red, hide-bound Chronicles were stored. The room was kept locked, and two dragons were needed in order to break the spell on the door.

Scordril paused in the doorway, realising guiltily that he had not taken enough interest in the Chronicles before. Large and heavy looking, the volumes were lined up on the wall opposite him. A few of the smartest bound books were apple-red with golden runes on their spines. These sat on a sturdy shelf cut into the rock itself. The rest stood on a very low, long trestle table below the shelf, stretching the width of the room. Made from planks of tree trunk, the table was thick and worn from years of use.

Scordril watched in fascination as Vanurl bent and ran his claws along the table, muttering aloud as he recalled the names of the Recorders and counted down the sun-rounds to the older Chronicles. »*In here is all the history of the times from the founding of Traprain until the Great Split. Of course, I was born at Traprain but I was young, not long past layring age when kin was divided. I did not understand. But I do remember how these were brought here. Fargelmir, Recorder at Traprain, allowed the Chronicles to come to Musselburgh for safekeeping, even though he remained at Traprain. Kvayn and her fellows ensured that they were smuggled out... This has always been the way that dragons keep their history. Perhaps that's why they are in trouble at Traprain now, they've lost their history...lost themselves...*« His voice trailed off and he stood for a moment lost in thought. It was the most Scordril had ever heard Vanurl say.

Then, reverently, Vanurl lifted an old volume from the far left-hand end of the table where the Chronicles seemed more frayed and the colour of their binding duller. He shuffled back and held the huge book out. »*Take this one, Scordril.*«

As the scent of dust and history filled the room, Scordril wondered how he could ever achieve his task. He wondered if Vanurl could help him. »*I have little time, Vanurl...*« He gazed down at the small, blue-grey dragon, over twice his age and into the wise green eyes that gazed back.

Vanurl tapped the volume of the Chronicles he'd given Scordril. »*In here! If there is an answer, you will find it here. Good night.*« And with that he turned and walked away.

Scordril stood still and ran his claws over the leather

on the book, feeling the scratches and dents of wear in the surface from over a century, more than 150 sun-rounds, of handling.

Then he settled himself on a smooth ledge against the wall and opened the book. Inside was page after page of thick paper, like a fine animal skin, all covered in perfect dragonscript. Here he would read about Jarl, the Great Split, and dragonmagic that could close like a noose at any time. Musselburgh might well be next. It would be a long night.

Still, it would be even longer for the Traprain Law dragons waiting to see if their messenger returned with help. Scordril thought of Gylning's long flight and the hopes of all the Traprain dragons hanging on it, and knew he must do what he could for his kin.

He took a deep breath and turned to the first page.

CHAPTER 2

The Chronicles - 1800

Lun-nau glow 4

Since the Lothian fishermen took over guarding the coast of the Great Forth River north of here, we have been honoured to help them in their watching. Nevertheless, we have seen no sign of invasion from overgrounder forces from France-across-the-sea, and begin to consider that the very great concern of the overgrounders was more dragonsnort than dragonfire. Nor have we seen signs of danger from elsewhere along the coast.

It is, therefore, with fear and trepidation that I record today three occasions when the fishermen have reported sighting strange, hovering shapes in the air above their boats at night. Shapes that wing in from the north and hover in the skies over Traprain Law and over the seas to the north where we rarely go, our feeding grounds being east and south-east of the layr. There is no noise, they say, but a strengthening of the wind in the vicinity of these shapes. They describe the hovering shapes as darker than grey but not black as the night.

The first occasion was at a point east of Bass Rock when a small fishing vessel was watching the coast to the south-east, down past Dunbar – for it is said that the invaders will sail this way up the coast in their large war vessels. While the fishermen watched, the leader – by name of Patrick Stobbs – reports that he felt a sudden cold breeze on his back, despite his heavy waterproof clothing, and that, on turning round, he saw a myriad hovering shapes. He cried out in fear and only just stopped his men from jumping overboard and swimming for their lives. However, he held on to his command of the crew and the shapes drew no nearer, but silently moved through the air like the dead at a vigil. After no more than five minutes of circling overhead, they turned into one 'fearsome mass' and winged off to the north. Patrick Stobbs is known among the coastal overgrounders as one of good renown, and his word can be believed.

The next occasion that has come to our notice was when our watchdragon, Ottvikk, went to join the watch and found a huddle of terrified fishermen at North Berwick, cowering behind a large rock on the headland while the shapes that had been terrifying them for several minutes 'winged away like a thousand gigantic black seagulls', according to the reports, far over the Isle of May and into the northern sea. Ottvikk himself did not see the shapes but he saw very well that brave and daring seamen had been turned into quivering overgrounders with little hope that they would survive the night. He believes that they were not hallucinating or influenced by the reports mentioned here that happened only one lun earlier, in lun-ok.

The final event – of such seriousness that I have decided to record all three here – is one that took place only last night at Skateraw harbour, east of Traprain. Here, the boats of the fleet were lined up snout to tail moving out of the harbour mouth to the sea. The night was dark and the lunar orb was hidden by mists and fog. They were about to set full sail when a great wind rose up from the north and rocked them till they thought they would be tipped to the bottom of the Great River. Byron Thurman, the night watch skipper, was sure that he felt a presence amid the wind and waves but was unable to make out anything for the great fog that surrounded them. He immediately called to the fishermen to heave to and return to the quay, where the general opinion was that the sudden storm had been caused by the same great dark shapes that had frightened the crews on other nights. They report that the presence was like when one of their kind has died and walks again. We do not understand this idea but our council has made a decision to increase the number of watchdragons...

Scordril turned forward a few more pages in his hurry to find out what happened – and then stopped suddenly, his gleaming sharp eyes caught by the word 'wingrider'. Whatever was a wingrider? He turned back a couple of pages to the beginning of the entry…

Lun-nau glow 20

Last night, another grave incident happened on the north foreshore. The dragons were helping the overgrounders according to our new arrangements, and dragons were on watch in three locations around the coast. North of here, the skipper Byron Thurman told Ottvikk that the night bore a breeze so gentle that the sails were hardly moving on their vessels. Thus, they were not planning to go too far out to sea on patrol because any intending invader would never be able to approach in such calm.

Ottvikk therefore decided to likewise patrol the near shore with his three youngones and teach them how to keep watch. He reports to the council that he saw no need to go on the wing himself since he could clearly see with dragonsight every detail, even the striped hats that Thurman's overgrounder men always wear. He also made the decision that they would morph into overgrounder shape in case the calm night brought overgrounders to the beach for one of their nightfires - as he calls them. This is apparently when they eat and drink and run up and down on the sandy foreshore. It does not happen much at this time in the sun-round but he was unwilling to take chances. We do not fear the overgrounders but in the main we keep ourselves away from all but the fishermen, who will not betray our confidence since they, too, have to trust us for help.

According to Ottvikk's report to the council, the breeze suddenly changed to a strong wind. He glanced up and caught sight of a vast hoard of winged beasts streaming in, dark and silent, across the night sky. He immediately called to his youngones and all four morphed and swept into the sky towards the mass of shadowy wings and heads, drawing fire from their bellies even as they winged upwards and outwards. Their intention was to scare off the incomers. But before they could arrive within fighting reach of the invaders, the outriders of the group had swooped down and, with their great wings, fanned waves so high that three vessels were immediately rendered upturned, throwing their occupants into the night swell.

Ottvikk declares that he saw quite clearly in that moment that the winged beasts were dragonkin. He is also adamant that they were similar in size and build to those of us who dwell here, but that their eyes were sunken and lacked the alert intelligence that marks a dragon who has drawn on magic. Just as the dark ones swooped back up from the wrecks of the vessels, he also noticed riders on each wing. Riders like overgrounders, but thin and bony, as if they had

22

not eaten in recent sun-rounds. One rider on each side, he reports, instead of one at the neck as we dragons would carry our riders. He referred to them as wingriders and nightdragons when discussing this event with the council, and those are the terms I shall use here for ease of description.

Ottvikk immediately trumpeted a battle call to summon any dragon within range. Many answered the call, emerging already half in flight from the northern tunnel, and rose to join him. But the vast hoard of nightdragons and their wingriders were even then ascending into the blackest part of the night.

Ottvikk decided that their chief duty was to the fishermen who had been capsized. These they rescued by plucking them from between the waves, which were already beginning to subside following the withdrawal of the nightdragons. The boats they could not save, however, for the ferocity of their capsizing had broken timbers and masts. Our dragons helped salvage the wood for the overgrounder hearths and parted with good wishes for a safe night until dawn. Their hearts are heavy, and ours too. For the dragon council is convinced that these winged visitors have been watching us and deliberately fermenting trouble. They may even have seen our tunnels and flightpaths. No one is safe while such an enemy abounds. Neither dragon nor overgrounder.

Lun-dek glow 15

There has been a breach of our defences. I now smell fear and unease as I move around the layr. The youngones are being kept safe from knowledge of these nightdragons and their wingriders, but their scales glow with a morbid tinge from time to time and I see that they are picking up from our minds the terror and tension that has invaded along with the night flyers. However, that is a matter for the dragoncouncil to see to. Here I will merely record the events of the last glow so that whatever happens to our layr as a result of this will be recorded for those who follow.

At sundown there was our usual conclave of the grown dragons, held every Lun-dek in the Great Cavehall to honour the memory of the ancestors who flew from the lands of the northmen in days of yore. Their bravery and courage at a time of immense need in their former homeland is always a cause of inspiration and renewed excitement for those of us who dwell in latter times. We do not willingly absent ourselves from this gathering. If the ancestors could endure whatever befell them, so can we in the years ahead. Therefore, it is with regret that I report here that we did not realise that the scheduled lone watchdragon would not be guard enough against a potential invasion such as came towards the end of our ceremony.

Braugnir raised the alarm with a violent scream and the conclave broke up immediately and rushed to the northern tunnel. Braugnir was already pushed back to the meeting of the tunnels which is directly below where the edge of the Law rises above our heads. I mention this, not because we do not know where this is, but to indicate to those who read this later that the invaders – who were a clawful of both nightdragons and wingriders – were already very far into our layr and spreading out in search of something. We do not know what. They had not killed Braugnir so we believe they were seeking something else, possibly something of value.

When the first rush of our dragons reached the tunnel meeting place, they were able with fire and mindmagic to repel the main group of invaders who were frightened and confused by our tactics.

We do not think they are like ourselves. Ottvikk's previous report of their sunken eyes was obviously true – and their black hides held a strange sheen in the darkness of our tunnels. However, they did not try to fight or use magic. It is possible, in Braugnir's opinion, that they were a small group sent to see how our layr is designed. As the main group left, Sygnadi – one of our quick-thinking growns – and Njortin, who has an excellent mind behind his long snout, went into the side tunnels in pursuit of any who had already passed inwards. They were followed by several other dragons. And, as they chased out the final stragglers - two nightdragons and their wingriders - they saw quite clearly that one wingrider had in his hand our sole remaining ancestral harness, studded with the wonderful jewels we have now lost the power to make. This attempted theft incensed the gathered dragons so much that they gave chase right to the end of the northern tunnel and onto the sands. They report that Braugnir caught the nearest nightdragon's tail in his snout and prevented the beast from soaring upwards, while Sygnadi leapt up at the thief-rider and snatched the harness from his hands. Njortin pointed out to the council afterwards that it would have been better to take the rider too and discover who they were and from where they come. However, the harness is back in our possession, apart from a small section that was torn loose in the fray. We have sent out search parties to the beach this morning but we fear that the tide from the Great River has taken a small part of our past into its jaws.

There is much discussion as to why the invaders would want the ancestral harness. They appear to have no magic, so it seems unlikely they would know about the darker magic that the ancestors wielded to make the jewels. There are some dragons - some of the mages, such as Kvakin who is old and wise - who are not so sure. Kvakin quizzed Njortin at length about something he had

26

overheard while chasing the remaining dragons from the tunnel. Njortin reports that the two nightdragons were mindspeaking just as we do. He caught fragments of speech that he understood among the many words that seemed to be in another dragonspeech entirely. 'Valuable metals' and 'power' and 'slaves' were the words that he remembers. He says that the nightdragons seem to be slaves of the wingriders. This is his deduction from hearing the fear and subservience in their mindvoices. Njortin has a brain that we do not ignore, so we have accepted this idea and are thinking about the meaning of it. Kvakin says that the valuable metals might refer to the jewels in the harness, though he does not know how they might have heard of the ancient magic stored within them. There is a dragonthought among the growns, whispered from one to another, that the wingriders have taken over the nightdragons and want also to take over the Traprain Law dragons by using their ancient artefacts. This seems far-fetched but is what is being said. Therefore I am recording it here.

Scordril let out a snort of anger as he turned the following pages, his sharp eyes carefully scanning over the more mundane entries about things important at the time but irrelevant to his present urgent quest. He stopped abruptly fifteen glows further on. The scribing here was just a little less careful. Fargelmir must have been agitated indeed not to take his usual care…

Lun-dek-en glow 2

It has not been possible for me to reach the Chronicles to update my recordings. For three glows we have been nursing our wounded, grieving for the dead and groaning for the damage done to the territory above our lair. Traprain Law looks as if dragonbreath has singed it, and of course it has. We are full of remorse for this damage done to the overgrounders' lands. Such a situation has never before arisen. Some of the fishermen know what has happened but we are confident they will not betray us to the overgrounders because of our alliance with them over the years. However, the betrayal that has been found here in our midst must be scribed so that all may know.

Scordil snorted again in frustration. Fargelmir knew what had happened – but if he only would get on and scribe it so that Scordril could understand, too!

Ottvikk is one of our wounded. He has been able to tell us that he was on watch duty during the night and noticed the rosy-fingered dawn creeping in from the east. I asked him to keep to the facts of the battle but his head is injured and he talks in a strange way when he is not dozing. He referred to the sea in the hours before the fight as 'wine-dark'. Wine is what the overgrounders make in their stills, he tells me: a deep red drink, 'as if stained by dragon blood'. In view of what happened next it seems important to me to record these words of the watchdragon, though they may be influenced by what happened as soon as the thick, woolly mist rolled in from the sea during the second half of the glow. After such a dragondream morning, we were much taken by surprise at this event and could not see our own snouts or tails. The hills became as white as the mageclouds we fly behind, and no one could see his next dragonneighbour as we hunted in the farms around for beasts to devour. That was how we did not see the nightdragons flying in from the north. They were not expected, as our experience has been that they fly by night in order to make up for the lack of mageclouding. The night hides them as if in the deepest cave. But the fog did too, this time, even though they are blacker than black.

The wingriders flew their dragons at us without warning. The layr emptied as we answered the call of those hunting above. From the youngest to the oldest, we knew that this was the moment we had feared. The battle was fierce with firebreath from both sides and a terrible clawing at scales and wings. At first, no dragon wanted to use more than the mildest mindmagic to put terror into the invaders – but soon Kvakin, senior among the mages, gave the order to use strong magics to form images of dragonhoards and mind-messages of reinforcements. I stayed on the outer edges of the Law using firebreath to repel nightdragons from where I thought the layr main entrance was. The fog and mist was so dense that I kept finding that

I had strayed west, but in my role as Recorder I knew that I had to be less brave and more observant than the others. I did what I could.

Kvakin reports to me that showing the images and sending messages to their minds seems to have made the wingriders frenzied. They flew amok round the Law, making their dragons fire the very ground under our wings. Some found the hidden entrances and tried to go in. Kvakin says they fought a battle of nerves because no dragon could use his dragonsight to penetrate the mist. It was claw-to-claw and fight when you found an enemy.

Never in the history of our layr do I recall such a sea-roke rolling in from the Great River. It lasted several glow-marks, according to the rather muffled overgrounder church bell in the fishing village, and at the end, when we thought the nightdragons and wingriders had been vanquished, there was a dreadful toll of injury and death. Among dragons that live so many sun-rounds, to find seven dead was a great distress. The keening and wailing lasted till evening, when we rose as one, high over the Great Forth River, and scattered their torched remains to the four winds. We knew the invaders would not return, for their injuries and losses were far greater. They had no magic to counter ours – and we do not feel one single dragonseye of remorse for that.

But our losses were not over. We returned to the

layr and surveyed the rubble of damaged entrances and tunnels, the torched land around us, and the nightdragon and wingrider carcasses scattered over a wide area. We torched those on the spot out of respect for our dragonkin because they are surely in thrall to the wingriders, who use them so badly. But the report then came to us at the dragoncouncil that Brekk, a smallone of less than one sun-round, was missing. We immediately sent search pairs into the tunnels, knowing that he must have strayed while the growns were occupied fighting. We were not at first worried. He might stray but he would not go out of the layr because smallones are not steady on their legs for many luns and their wings do not carry them except in hops and jumps. Besides, he would be greatly frightened by what he could hear of the battle above and around him. So we searched with hope.

It was only later that Sygnadi called us to council again and told us what he had discovered. (It is a matter of shame to me to report the events that occurred here. But the facts must be told so that others may read and note.) Sygnadi and his younger sibling, Jarl, were searching to the east, in the tunnels whose entrances were most damaged during the battle. Sygnadi asserted that he could smell Brekk's smallone scent and that they should follow it as far as possible. Shortly afterwards, they came to a joining of the ways and communicated together as to which way they would go, since the scent was *less obvious. When Sygnadi decided that they should take the right-claw tunnel, where there was some piling of rubble fallen from the roof, Jarl claimed that this was now worse than before. In this way, Sygnadi reports with scorn, Jarl gave away that he had been there during the battle or directly in its aftermath. Sygnadi admits he threatened the youngone with fiery violence if he didn't tell him exactly what he knew. Turning on one's dragonkin is wrong as a general rule but these were serious events. Jarl then broke down and told his brother what he had done and it is this that I wish to record here, although I can hardly bring myself to do so, knowing it will be told in dragonhistory for all time.*

Scordil shut his eyes momentarily, as if to avoid reading what came next. Then he moved his cramped body and blew a gentle dragonbreath over his scales. A chill had enveloped him that was not connected with the lateness of the hour. Something very bad was about to be revealed…

Jarl had prowled around the layr as soon as the fighting began to die down. He had not been involved in the aerial battle but in the guarding of the layr entrances. When he was no longer needed, he felt angry at what had happened and set about viewing the damage. However, he neglected to take a companion dragon with him and found himself in the eastern limits of the layr on his own. Here he found Brekk, injured beyond help by a fall of rocks that had caught his wings. The smallone was breathing but unconscious. Knowing he could not live, Jarl was about to torch him when he was confronted by two wingriders with their nightdragon.

Not sensing where he could draw on magepower at that moment to protect himself, and having only fire and claws to fight with, he knew he was outnumbered. He pleaded for his life. This was cowardly for a dragon but he is still young. Speaking through the mind of the nightdragon, the wingrider who was in charge prevented his companion from killing Jarl and demanded instead the body of the 'dead dragon'. Jarl knew that Brekk was unconscious rather than dead, but told Sygnadi that he knew the smallone would be dead within a very short time, such were his injuries. He therefore agreed to the exchange – his life for the body of Brekk – and the wingriders moved forward to take Brekk. As they pulled the body away from the rock that trapped his wing, Jarl heard Brekk's last breath leave his body. He therefore thought that the exchange did not matter, he says. Sygnadi has told him in no uncertain dragonspeech that such an action was despicable and unworthy of dragonkin; that Brekk's ashes should have been scattered to the four winds, as is our custom.

The result is that sharp discussion has arisen among us about Jarl's action. The discussion has been held in closed council with only the leaders and mages present, as our understanding is that it might increase the damage if Jarl's true actions became apparent throughout the layr. No one disputes the error of Jarl's action. But some among us feel that it was the action of a youngone who has yet to learn to think under fire. Others believe that even Jarl, only fifty sun-rounds old, should have remembered that the wingriders had already tried to steal a harness. He should have been ready to think further than the end of his thick snout. Even as I sit recording this entry in our Chronicles, word is passing round the layr that Jarl is a traitor, that he betrayed his people. Others believe this without knowing what happened. Only we on the council know the true story and even we cannot agree among ourselves as to exactly what Jarl was thinking when he did this dreadful deed. Some of the mages think it might be better if we told the full details of Jarl and Brekk to the dragonclan instead of trying to keep it quiet. I record this fact here for you who read later to decide.

Scordil passed over the next few pages. There was obviously nothing important written on them. The entries were short and factual, and Fargelmir's script had returned to the measured lettering he always used. Catching sight of Ottvikk's name once more, in an entry nearly two luns later, he paused and resumed reading…

Lun-dek-tri glow 20
Ottvikk, now much recovered from his injuries, has found something startling on his flights to the north.

As he returned from his hunting trip two glows ago, he was unable to fly straight towards the northern entrance. He said that there was something stopping him. He could not explain what it was, just that the air would not let him through. At first, he made a detour of several wingspans to the right and entered the Law by that means. However, later he claims he was too puzzled by the incident to concentrate on his layr watch duties, so, leaving Braugnir in charge of the watch dragons, he returned to the place where this strange piece of air had been. He snouted around for a while until he found it again and then drew on magepower from Njortin in order to rend the phenomenon asunder. However, on turning back, he found that he could not exit from that point – as if the air had reverted to how it had been. He returned to the watch via a different route and reported this to the council that night.

In addition, Kvayn, a bright, intelligent, newly grown dragon, reports that she was unable to access the hidden door in the heathland to the east. This door is seldom used but she is adamant she was in the right place and the door refused to open to her. She has only just come into her mage power and is yet to become fully aware of it – she is not on the council for this reason – and it may be that she should have drawn on Njortin's own power to open the entrance. It is a worrying sign, however.

Lun-en glow 10
There have been further incidents concerning entering

the layr. Braugnir has been unable to enter, just as Ottvikk could not, only this time it was from the south. And Jarl, too, reports that he found his way blocked from the south-east by something that was denser than air, almost as if an invisible dragon were there pushing against him, he said. Already there have been dragons saying amongst themselves that it would be better if Jarl had been shut out forever. But we on the council are more concerned with finding out what is happening to Traprain Law and have arranged for the mages among us to inspect these anomalies and find out what we can.

Lun-en glow 21

A meeting of the magecouncil was called tonight, attended by Njortin, whose sense of leadership in this matter spills out from his swirling eyes; Harmin (mother of Braugnir), Gullfi and Skolfari (the young twins who are already into their mage strength); Kvakin (the oldest) and myself, Fargelmir, as Recorder. The mages were debating together on the findings of their excursion to inspect the sites where the anomalies have been found. The facts to be recorded here are that these places seem to be set in some kind of circle around Traprain Law – around the layr, in fact – and that with their mage senses, they are sure that there are traces of magic at each site. However, the strange thing is that this is no full-blown remnant of power but an embryonic trace, such as might be left by a youngone who has not yet realised his or her powers. Njortin suggested that this might stem from the missing piece *of the harness and that perhaps the wingriders had managed to take and use it in some way. Kvakin disputes this, saying that he has worked with the remnants of older magic for so long that he would know that scent anywhere. The traces must be of their own magic, however strange it appeared.*

At this point, the twins spoke together and almost deafened us with their roar of fury. Their idea is that the smallone Brekk, who was lost at the time of the nightdragon attack, might have had mage power yet to be recognised, so young was he. This, they claim, would mean that the wingriders could use it as a weapon against the layr, even though they had no magic of their own. Njortin thought that this would mean that they had not yet become sophisticated in its use and that this explained why the Traprain Law dragons could counteract it to a certain extent. Gullfi was adamant that there was more to it than that. But no one has come up with another explanation yet. The realisation that the loss of Brekk was not only dishonourable and possibly treacherous, but also something that has possibly brought a terrible disaster in its wake, makes my heart heavy to record it.

Something was nagging at the back of Scrodril's mind, but he was so near the end of the volume that he read on, his eyelids drooping with tiredness and worry. What he needed to know was why the Great Split finally happened, and then perhaps he could try to put it all together and sort out what must be done.

Lun-to glow 6

There are renewed arguments among us about Jarl, Brekk and a possibly growing danger. We try to keep the true story of Brekk under dragon-skin so that tempers will not be needlessly excited. We cannot afford to have a deep schism. However, some dragons are saying that we should have more links with overgrounders, not fewer. (We have stopped helping the fishermen, who understand that we have an emergency of our own to deal with.) Others say that it was by going out to help the fishermen that the nightdragons and wingriders found our presence here. And that we should withdraw even more from contact with overgrounders. The scornful among this faction have been heard to ask if the others honestly think they can negotiate with such as the wingriders, who have already conquered a dragon race. This is a dark moment for the clan.

Lun-to glow 24

The group that is going to Musselburgh is about to leave. Once there, they will found another layr and run it their own way. There is bad feeling but much silence. We have never had such an occurrence in our history. A split is a great dishonour to dragonkin. I have, with sadness of heart, agreed that the group will take the official Chronicles up to and including this last entry. I shall continue in another journal, but although my heart is heavy with emotion, I believe that the Chronicles will be safer there than here, while this threat hovers over our lair. I shall miss the youngones and newly grown, such as Ygdrann and Vanurl – Ygdrann is growing into magepower these last months. Vanurl is a dragon after my own kind, interested in facts and records, always popping in to snout among the very old ones. I have kept the later ones from him so that the truth about Jarl will remain hidden – now it seems good to have done that. Then at least they will not be read until they are well away from here. I am sad at the departure of Kvayn, my dragonmate's young friend, for she is alert and lively in our lair. Sygnadi stays because Jarl is his kin and nobody wishes to take Jarl to the new lair. I shall not so totally miss the grown who are leaving, for the youngones are those who truly hold my heart...

CHAPTER 3

Traprain Law - 1950

The layr was eerily quiet as Scordril closed the large Chronicle and laid it carefully to one side on the ledge. He was tired and his mind whirled. He felt as if his head would explode if all the thoughts flying around collided. With a sigh, he made himself more comfortable, stretching his legs and tail out in front of himself, and began to reflect on the many things he had learned.

Clearly, something had been wrong at Traprain for some time. Even before the move to Musselburgh. But the Chronicles indicated that it was not the ancestors of the Traprain dragons who had created the spells. The problems had only begun at the time of Fargelmir the Recorder. So, Scordril reasoned, if strange magic that blocked the way into the Traprain layr had been noted all that time ago, yet Gylning had only come for help now, it must mean that the magic had grown more powerful with the passing of time. In other words, the magic seemed to have matured and closed around the layr like snapping jaws. That worried Scordril. He couldn't think of any ordinary dragonmagic that would behave like that, or take so long to develop. It had to be the sort of powerful, dark magic that the ancients used to fashion their treasures, tools and precious jewels. Or the kind of magic a very powerful mage could possess…

Scratching his snout, Scordril thought instead about the nightdragons. If he hadn't read the accounts in the Chronicles, he may not have believed that such dragons existed. Of course, there were tales of ferocious beasts, fearsome overgrounders with cruel weapons, told around the fires on long winter nights. But he'd always thought that they were only tales told to scare the youngones. Never in a million sun-rounds would he have guessed that such things were really exaggerated facts. The thought of nightdragons with loathsome, controlling wingriders made him shiver to the very tip of his tail. Why had the nightdragons visited Traprain anyway? Was it really to find treasure, like the ancestral harness they tried to steal? Or was it something more sinister like enslaving the Traprain dragons? He tried to think. The answer wasn't easy, yet it must be there in the Chronicles he'd just read.

He tried to slot all the pieces together but something was missing. What could have brought invaders not just once but twice? Twice – that was a terrible thought. What if they still weren't satisfied, hadn't found what they wanted, and came a third time? Scordril stared into the dimness of the room, and snorted tiny flames of coloured light for company.

That was all history, he told himself sternly. I must think of the present and the trapped dragons. What to do to save them? The most difficult thing would be to work out how he could bring together all the dragons in the rescue of those at Traprain. Many of the dragons alive at Musselburgh had left Traprain after the Great Split. The bitterness that was written about in the Chronicles over Jarl's behaviour, when Brekk was lost, had even passed down through the next generation of dragons – to those who hadn't been at Traprain at the time. Scordril considered it a great pity that dragons, even mages, could be so obstinate at times over things they didn't really know about. Dragons like Fenror, who seemed to have absorbed his father's well-known dislike of the Traprain dragons. Whatever had happened in the past, the Traprain dragons did not deserve what had happened to them, he reasoned.

Scordril decided that his first job would have to be to convince the council that the rescue was justified. And that would be very soon, in just two glow-marks. He had better get at least a tiny portion of sleep. So he yawned and curled up as much as he could, rested his head upon his arm, and fell asleep dreaming of doors that appeared then vanished with a snap.

———❦———

The campsite at the foot of Traprain Law had stirred from its short but chilly night. People milled around, keen to get to work. Set slightly apart from the main field were a couple of single-person canvas tents, like miniature barns supported by two poles. Drops of dew still beaded their roofs.

'Let's get out of here,' Flick pleaded. 'I hate hanging round.'

Morris glanced over at her and grinned at the sight of his cousin's flushed face. Her hazel eyes gleamed in the bright sunlight. She idly kicked at a tent peg and ran her fingers through her tangle of red-blond curls, flicking her head sharply to one side as if to discourage a pesky fly. This was why she was known as Flick instead of by her proper name, Felicity, and it was a sure sign she was frustrated.

The early morning mist that had been hovering over the small group of tents had now lifted, and the sun was shining. Morris, too, wanted to be off.

'We'd be quicker if you helped with this bedroll,' he said. 'How come I have to tidy both tents while you hang around like a lazy dog? Aren't girls supposed to make beds?'

'Not this girl,' Flick retorted. 'And anyway, who was it who walked all the way in that disgusting early-morning mist to the village just so you could have milk on your cereal? I've done my bit.'

Morris hauled the second roll of sleeping bag and pyjamas onto the crudely lashed sticks that kept them off the ground during the day. If they didn't do this now, they'd pay for it tonight when the bedding was damp and chilly. He had already dragged both groundsheets out and spread them upside down in the sun to dry. His dad was strict about letting the grass breathe underneath the tents.

'Going home,' he said slowly, 'is a treat. Your dad probably gave you some sweets from the shop's rations – which you've probably forgotten to tell me about.'

'He didn't, too!' Flick's slightly grubby face took on a look of pure indignation. She acted more like a boy than most of the ones in his class. Then she grinned. 'He did give me this, though.' She held out the latest Beano comic as if it were a prize.

Morris groaned. 'You're not having the torch on all night like last week,' he said. 'I couldn't get to sleep for this great thing shining in my face like an enemy searchlight through the tent walls.' He fumbled to roll back and tie up the door of his own tent and then stood up. 'That's finished now. Where are we going?'

Flick folded the comic carefully until it was smaller than a postcard, then stuffed it into the back pocket of her shorts where it looked very like a jack-in-the-box waiting to get out. 'Up to the top?' she asked.

'What a surprise!' said Morris. 'I mean, we could always run up, or maybe crawl up or hop there, just to make it different to yesterday… Flick – what do two magpies mean?'

Flick looked puzzled. 'I know it's silly of me, but I didn't think this tiny amount of sun was enough to turn your head. What are you talking about?'

Morris pointed over Flick's head. 'Look! Magpies circling over the Law.'

Flick spun round and stared. 'Joy, I think. I've heard Mum quote it. One for sorrow, two for joy. It's an old rhyme – but they're going now. At least they've got some sense. No point in standing here doing nothing. Come on!'

'We're not doing nothing,' said Morris mildly. 'We're watching magpies.'

44

Flick cuffed him with his own pullover, which she'd been about to hand him. 'It might come cold. Don't want to freeze to death up there.'

Morris slipped it on quickly. They looked like twins now in their green jumpers and grey shorts and almost equally short hair. 'We'll have to tell them first or they'll send us home for breaking rules,' he said, nodding towards the main area of the camp where Morris's parents and a group of other archaeologists were working on a dig.

'If they send me home, you can come too,' said Flick obstinately. 'We could still explore the hill together. It's only a mile from our shop.'

Morris shook his head. He wanted to stay on site. It was fun camping. He was enjoying the sort of freedom he never had at home. They'd come over in the car, piled with all the packs and equipment, almost as soon as term finished in Musselburgh. They'd pitched their own small tents a little distance from the others so they could be private, doing all their own cooking, deciding their own bedtimes and looking after themselves. Not that they washed much. It was a long walk to the stream so they brought a bucket of water up to the camp and splashed their faces in it every morning. If it ran out, they went back for more. He was enjoying himself.

His parents were hoping to find something as important as the Roman spoons someone had found many years ago. He'd spent the first few days helping them and had been excited to find all sorts of small rocks, pebbles and shards of what looked like pottery. His parents had been rather dismissive. 'It's not what we're looking for,' his mum had said. 'You can tell what's important if you know about these things.'

Now, when faced with the two cousins, she just said, as she always did, 'Make sure you take care up there. It's a big drop if you fall off.'

Morris was pretty sure she wasn't much bothered what they did, so long as they didn't get hurt or stay away too long. She'd been quite keen for Flick to join them when she found they were to be so near Traprain village. 'It'll be good for them to get to know each other better,' she'd said when his father had protested that Morris would be bored and Flick even worse.

Actually, he wasn't bored with the dig because he liked the idea of finding out what ancient people used to live like. Chipping away at the hardened soil with a little pickaxe, sifting through the stones and earth, made him feel like an explorer. But he did like being with Flick, too. So, whooping like two cowherds, they shouted their goodbyes and charged over the grass towards the slope of the Law that was easiest to climb up.

'Beat you,' Flick called over her shoulder. 'Sloooowcoach!'

'No one said anything about a race,' Morris protested. Days spent with Flick were like fairground rides, dashing this way and that.

When they were only about a third of the way up, Flick, who had been running all over the place instead of marching straight up the hill like Morris, called to him, 'Hey, look here!'

'What now?' Morris paused and held out his arm for a butterfly to land on. While he enjoyed the ticklish sensation on his arm, he looked over to where Flick was excitedly jumping up and down and pointing.

'It's a gap. Come on! Quick!'

Morris gently blew the butterfly on its way and ran over to her, his canvas shoes slipping on the still damp grass. 'Whadya mean, a gap?' he said, slithering to a halt.

The place Flick stood staring at was a gently raised area, where a very large boulder was set into the mound as if blocking a hole.

'It's nothing,' said Morris, disappointed. 'The grass has just pulled away over the years. I thought you meant a real gap and a real tunnel behind it. Come on, let's get up on top. We could fly your plane. Have you got it with you?'

Flick often had a tiny cardboard speed-demon bomber with her – almost as if she imagined herself as the wartime pilot her dad had been. They usually took it in turns to wind up the rubber band and see how far it flew, testing out angles and different wind directions.

'Course I have,' said Flick, absently. 'But I think this rock would move. Let's try it— Oh all right. Bagsy me the first turn then.'

On top, there was a breeze that made their experiments with the plane too difficult to manage so they mooched around for a while kicking pebbles. Then Flick started throwing them in different ways and challenged Morris to make his land on top, as if playing marbles. They were by now well over to the west and – Morris suspected – nearer to the vertical drop than his mother would approve of. 'Careful,' he warned.

'There's not many ledges to catch you if you fall.' He took aim and threw his pebble after Flick's. It bounced and slithered past a standing rock.

'Yah! Missed me by miles!' shouted Flick. 'I'll easily get yours now.' She picked up hers and lobbed it – right over the outcrop of rock that was probably part of the former fortifications. It made a strange thump several seconds before it should have touched the ground. She stared back at Morris in alarm. 'D'ya hear that?' she said in a hoarse whisper. 'It landed on something else.'

'Not a sheep, I hope,' said Morris, sprinting over.

They peered round the stone. Morris caught his breath sharply.

—✿✿✿—

The magecouncil had gathered and was waiting for Scordril as he entered the Great Hall. They turned to look as he slowly took his seat before the fire pit. The lonely place of a speaker, instead of his normal seat alongside the other mages.

Kvayn sat with her hands on her knees, her tail flicking gently back and forward beside her. »*Well? You have read the Chronicles. Do you bring us an answer, Scordril?*»

»*Gylning speaks the truth. I am sure of that,*» said Scordril, glancing around the mages seated before him. He wondered how Gylning was, but could see that the others were only eager to learn what he had read. »*Even before Fargelmir passed the Chronicles to Musselburgh, strange things were noted. Dragonmagic that no longer worked. Even you are reported as noticing, Kvayn... A time is recorded when you apparently could not enter by a door in the heathland.*»

»*True enough. I dreamed of my younger days last night, and that was one memory that came to me. I wasn't alone in noticing.*» Kvayn nodded wisely, as if agreeing with herself. »*But there is more? I sense it and see the worry in your eyes, Scordril.*»

»*Like explaining why we should help them?*» Fenror snorted, clearly ready to be as difficult as he had been the previous glow.

Scordril struggled to hold his rising temper in check. »*Yes. Much more! Things we must talk of now. To decide how best to act. And act we must, for I have read of magic, battles, Jarl, the Great Split... and of nightdragons.*» Scordril felt as if his words hung in the air in front of him, like a magecloud might if it could look like words.

»*Nightdragons?*» Ygdrann's dark face seemed to have frozen into a picture of alertness. He turned away from Scordril and looked at Kvayn. »*Their damage was great. Have they left so much hatred behind that they poison the very magic around Traprain? I cannot bear to hear of them, if so. My father was one of those lost in the battle for Traprain.*» Ygdrann's skin seemed to grow paler. His eyes flashed with silver lights of distress.

Kvayn's eyes looked bright. »*Calm your fear, Ygdrann. Hear Scordril out as he speaks of the Chronicles' worst tales. I, for one, wish to know the truth about Jarl and the Great Split. If only to rule out the possibility of a trap.*»

»*I saw no reasons for a trap as I read,*» Scordril

answered, looking straight at Fenror as he spoke. »*And I cannot speak of Jarl without telling the tale of the nightdragons.*»

He then tried to summarise the events that surrounded the appearance of the nightdragons. How they had frightened the fishermen. Then forced their way into Traprain layr, snatched the ancient harness and been repelled. Only to return in force and mount a surprise attack. And how dragon had had to fight dragon in order to survive. He told the others about the recorded thoughts that perhaps the nightdragons did not possess any magic and were slaves to the wingriders. Crucially, he also suggested that the 'overheard talk' about the 'valuable metals', 'power' and 'slaves' was a plan of the wingriders, who would doubtless return to capture the Traprain dragons.

The rest of the council sat and listened intently. From time to time Kvayn held her claws up to stop any questions, nodding for Scordril to continue.

Scordril tried to sound calm, but inside his pulse raced. He saw and sensed how the others were disturbed by the tale. »*So you see, the loss of Brekk, in the midst of the battle, led to the Great Split. Jarl was either foolish or acted knowingly, as a traitor might. I could not say for sure. Fargelmir, the Recorder, was as fair and honest as Kvayn said he would be. The only dragon to know for sure would be Jarl himself.*»

»*So, we are to rescue dragonkin when one of their number could do such a terrible thing! Even if Jarl is long gone, what if there are more of his type?*» Fenror half rose as his voice grew louder and louder.

Scordril could contain his anger and impatience no longer. This was exactly what he had feared would happen and it would get them nowhere. Arching his back, he snorted red-hot flames of disgust into the air, leaving a smell of burning in his nostrils. »*It was one young dragon who knew no better! Battle was raging through the layr. His very life was threatened. I say again, only Jarl knew why he did this thing. We should be mage-like and see the fullness of the tale.*»

Kvayn's leathery wings rustled behind her as she braced her shoulders. Then she unfolded them, flapping them back against the wall. The slapping sound echoed round the hall. »*Silence! That is not important here!*» Kvayn's voice sounded shrill in Scordril's mind. He winced with headpain. »*What is, is the fact that the Chronicles say nightdragons seemed to have no magics. Why, then, did a barrier appear? What is generating this magic? Why has it grown in strength? Can we remove its power?*»

»*And how?*» Ygdrann added loudly.

Scordril tried to think before he spoke. »*The answer to that is unclear. Even the magecouncil at Traprain, when the anomalies first occurred, could not be sure why it appeared. Some thought it related to the magic in the ancestral harness that was almost stolen. Others believed it related directly to Brekk, the lost youngone, perhaps destined to be a mage. Whatever the source is, it lies somewhere in Traprain layr itself or the area around the Law.*»

Kvayn rocked gently on her seat. »*An ancient magic, but from where? Matured with time, but no one knows why.*» Her quiet voice sounded like a youngone playing at riddles.

»*So what should we do?*» Fenror asked in a more cooperative tone.

Ygdrann spoke up confidently. »*If it is ancient magic, mage power that has matured, then the only way to defeat it is to use more ancient magic! Use like against like.*»

Fenror frowned. »*As Threah uses in her treatment of some illness?*»

»*Exactly!*» said Ygdrann, nodding vigorously.

»*But how are we to use ancient Traprain magic? We have none!*» Fenror flushed a deeper purple as he spoke. »*It's pointless, anyway, as the ancients had difficulty controlling their own magic. That's partly why the knowledge was lost. It isn't easy to control!*»

»*And what if using the magic attracts the nightdragons?*» Scordril said. He felt his mind returning to the Chronicles as he asked.

»*The barrier exists now. Why doesn't that attract the nightdragons?*» said Kvayn, looking around her at the other mages, as if testing them for their answer.

»*It might,*» Fenror suggested. »*But they come from far away. Maybe they've all died, or forgotten about Traprain.*»

»*The Chronicles said that nightdragons are not like us. What if they live for much longer?*» said Scordril, suddenly realising that this was why he'd been fearful that they would return.

»*Maybe they've been scouting already, even here and we don't know it...*» Ygdrann looked aghast as he spoke. »*Surely we must prepare for war. We cannot let this layr be taken by a surprise attack.*»

»Yes. We must work on our magic to protect

ourselves. *Take the hatchlings and youngones to the deepest part of the layr. Relearn the ways of our warrior ancestors!*» Fenror thrashed his tail around as he spoke.

Kvayn clashed her claws together. »*Enough! We cannot say anything for sure unless we speak with the Traprain dragons. To do that, we must rescue them. In turn, we must find out whether we can even get through the barrier. And maybe to do that we need some ancient item from Traprain. A dilemma indeed.*»

Scordril rose up from his seat. »*I suggest that I fly to Traprain and inspect things for myself. I will return before this glow is over and we can meet again.*» Scordril hid his doubts within the deepest parts of his mind and tried to send a feeling of confidence to the other mages.

»*I agree, Scordril.*» Kvayn turned to look at Ygdrann and Fenror in turn. They nodded. »*It is the only way we will know how things are. Speak with Gylning before you leave. He is much recovered already. Threah is caring for him well. One of us will follow behind you towards Traprain but will stop at a point on the boundary of our hunting lands when mindspeech becomes impossible. The two remaining here will take turns to work a dragonspell to strengthen the power of any mindlink. That way, if you are in danger you may still have a chance to link to us. Meanwhile, I will mobilise this layr to prepare for a war we hope will not happen.*»

Kvayn signalled the close of the meeting by rising to her feet. »*Good hunting.*»

—◦◦◦—

Scordril hurried to visit Gylning. Although he was keen to be off and flying to Traprain Law, he knew that he needed to find out more from the young messenger. He couldn't simply blunder into the unknown. He knew nothing about the area around the layr there. He didn't want to end up trapped himself. He told himself it wouldn't happen because his magepower was very strong. But in the back of his mind he imagined nightdragons and wingriders and was wary.

He entered the room in which Glyning lay recovering, still on his lying-stone. He sniffed the air and smelled flowers – no doubt Threah's ointments. He saw that one of Gylning's wings was bandaged up and that both sets of his claws were wrapped, too.

Threah rose from her cushion in the corner of the room. She smiled to see Scordril.

»*Welcome, Scordril.*» Threah greeted him in a low voice. »*Gylning is resting but he is much better. You need to speak with him?*»

»*Yes. I must fly to Traprain Law and investigate the magic. To find the barrier if it exists. And if it does, to find a way of breaking its power.*»

»*Traprain?*» Gylning's young voice sounded tired. »*I will go with you. You will need a guide.*»

»*You shall do no such thing, youngone!*» Threah glared at Gylning, and then Scordril, as she spoke. »*Let him answer your few questions, but he is not fit to fly.*»

Scordril almost grinned. The emphasis had been so clear in Threah's tones that he would not keep Gylning long. And so he made his questions as brief as possible.

He wanted to know where Gylning thought he should

look for the strange magic. The youngone also explained the location of the entrances to the layr, just in case. And most interestingly, and perhaps critical, Scordril thought, he mentioned for the very first time that animals and birds, and even the occasional human, seemed free to stray across Traprain Law without any problem. Scordril smiled as the glimmer of an idea formed. Perhaps a dragon morphed as an overgrounder would be safe to come and go.

Scordril turned to leave. Gylning looked distressed but Threah was right, he was not strong enough to move. Besides, his wing would take a while to heal. Scordril promised Gylning he would return as soon as possible with news.

———◦/◦/◦———

Ygdrann flew part of the way with Scordril and listened to the new information from Gylning, which suggested overgrounders could pass through the barrier without any problem. Then, as Kvayn had ordered, he stopped at the boundary of the Musselburgh dragons' land.

Scordril flew on, protected from overgrounder view by his magecloud, and following a mixture of Gylning's and Ygdrann's directions. The sun warmed his back as he flew and it wasn't long before he could see Traprain Law rising up in the distance, like a beached whale. When he judged it right, he gently came down to land. He rubbed his claws nervously: the answer to all his questions lay up ahead.

He took a deep breath, drew on his mage strength

and changed into overgrounder form. It was a long time since he'd morphed in this way and he always worried that he would choose clothing that made him look ridiculous. He had kept a sharp dragonseye on the overgrounders he had seen in the distance when on hunting trips, but he had no wish to look like an old farmer herding cattle. Instead, he'd tried to look as an overgrounder might if he came to Traprain to walk: a pair of tough boots, thick grey socks and dark green loose trousers seemed suitable. His pale grey and green checked shirt, with the sleeves rolled up was a guess.

He knew from his observations that overgrounders seemed to have a love of walking across places just like Traprain. Usually with heavy weights on their backs and even carrying sticks. When he was younger, he'd wondered if they needed the sticks to fight off other overgrounders, or to burn for warmth. But he'd never seen either of these things happen. Besides, Scordril doubted that they would need them on such a warm summer day. The sun was already high in the sky. His normal scales would have been shimmering.

Scordril looked around him, his deep brown eyes wary, his short, dark hair ruffled slightly by the gentle breeze. He'd given himself a distance to walk to the Law itself because it would let him circle round the area of the Traprain dragons' layr. Besides, if he'd gone nearer as a dragon, he couldn't be sure that overgrounders wouldn't be around. He didn't know this area. And Gylning had only explained the few things that he'd been asked or thought essential.

So, with all his senses alert, Scordril started slowly and

methodically walking in his sturdy hiking boots towards the hill, the Law itself. Towards the place where Gylning had told him there was an entrance. The place where he would put an entrance if he were a Traprain mage.

He might not be able to fly or breath fire while he was morphed, but he still had all his keen magepower and his five senses, so he sought any trace of dragonkin with his magesight. Listening for a distant call. Sniffing the air every few minutes. Then he reached an area of ground where his skin prickled. All his dragon senses were suddenly alert. The small hairs on the back of his human neck stood on end.

He concentrated very hard and took a single step forward. He felt the air push gently against him, like a strange wall of water suspended between the sky and the ground. But there was nothing to be seen. He looked from side to side and saw nothing. This was what he'd read about and what the council had discussed. He pushed back against it. An overgrounder would hardly notice the strange effect, but Scordril knew the air resisted him, until his hands went through the thin spongy layer and out the other side. He tried a foot and then the other one, and, to his surprise, his body followed. He felt as if he were walking through a thick curtain. He stepped back and the air returned to fill the space he had taken up, like a gigantic stretched sheet of rubber springing back to its true shape. Nervously, he stuck out his tongue and gulped it back again. He could taste magic. Pushing against the air, he stepped to his right and tasted the air again. Once again, he tasted the unmistakable bitter tang of old magic, like…

Another step, then another taste, then again. Soon he had located a long stretch of the curving boundary of magic that Gylning had spoken of. Inside himself he shivered despite the baking-hot sun. He could see the hill of the Law in front of him. The hill and the Traprain dragons were without doubt on the inside of the barrier if it continued as Gylning described.

Scordril wanted to see how far the boundary stretched but decided it would be a waste of his short visit. So he made straight for the Law. Once there, he started to climb up so that he could look down to see the land on the other side without walking all the way around. As he climbed, he thought hard.

The barrier could not have appeared by chance. Dragonmagic had to be put there by a dragon. The logical thing was the nightdragons, as the Chronicles had suggested. But that meant they'd got their magic from somewhere. The dragons in the Chronicles had wondered if it might be connected with the harness, or if smallone Brekk might have had undiscovered magepower. That was almost certainly the truth. And that meant that this strange magic he had tasted on his tongue was probably a mixture of ancient and modern magic, maturing into something they could only hope to find an antidote to. And meanwhile, Njortin, the dragonmaster, and all his dragons were without food and water and perhaps even air: who knew if air could pass through the magic barrier round the entrances?

He pressed on upwards until the ground levelled out at the top, where he paused. Over to his left he could see the whole expanse of the Forth, broad as several dragon layrs as it widened to the ocean. It was a view he'd seen many times from the air, so he gave it little attention. But from here, too, he could see the land on the other side of the Law. He moved towards the edge of the steep drop to the south. The sound of the stony ground crunching under his feet as he walked was suddenly replaced by the sound of overgrounder voices. His keen sight saw that there were a dozen or more far below on the grassy land. Then he saw tents. By dragons' teeth, there was a small village of people living just below the foot of the Law on the other side!

Scordril wanted to fly down and walk right up to the overgrounders and demand to know what they were doing. That would be stupid – he couldn't blow his cover. Instead he settled himself down on the ground, where he wouldn't be as noticeable and concentrated on the strange sight. The overgrounders seemed to be making holes in the earth. Crawling all around them like ants seeking food. Whatever could they be looking for?

Scordril sat for a long while, but the activity still made no sense. Were they mining for something? Hunting for dragons? He told himself not to be so silly. He tried again to sense dragons but couldn't.

Eventually he got up, turned away and began to climb back over the hill towards the opposite side, away from the strange earthworks. He was weary now. He couldn't keep up the morphed appearance for much longer and he knew it. *How the overgrounders manage without flying, I cannot imagine,* Scordril thought to himself. His legs felt like sacks of stones dragging with every step.

He sank down onto a grassy bump, protected from the sun by a protruding rock, like the stump of a wall, and stared out over the heathland and his way home.

A sudden noise startled Scordril. A sliver of stone bounced past his shelter. The next one hit his head.

CHAPTER 4

The Camp

The man sitting in front of Morris and Flick was leaning against the rock and rubbing his head. But his face was puzzled rather than angry.

'Hello, sir,' said Morris quickly. 'We're really sorry. It was a game, an accident. We didn't mean—'

Flick added her own apology. 'Sorry, sir.' She smiled at him sweetly – something that made her seem very childish, Morris thought, rather than the tough tomboy she always presented.

The stranger looked like a walker, taking a rest after climbing up the hard way. Maybe if they talked to him, he would see they hadn't meant to hit him. 'Are you new here? Lots of people come to see this place. It's very old—'

'My dad says it used to be called Dunpender,' Flick interrupted, 'which means a steep hill, which is sort of why people get tired climbing up.'

Morris flashed her a grateful smile. She was always quick to cotton on. He grinned his best grin and was relieved when the stranger's face relaxed and the man said, a bit uncertainly, 'I am a visitor, yes. My name is Roderick.'

'I'm Morris and this is my cousin Flick – Felicity. We're camping near the dig. In tents. It's school holidays, you know, and my parents are hoping to find treasure.'

'Not that what they find will be worth anything,' said Flick. 'It's rubbish trying to piece together how people lived from bits of bone and pottery and things.'

Roderick pulled himself slowly to his feet. He was quite a bit taller than them but stooped as if weary. Morris thought he looked very tired for someone who was dressed like a real hiker.

'Are you okay, sir?' he asked anxiously. 'The stone...'

'Yes, yes. But this dig, the people in those tents?'

'My parents and their friends. They're archaeologists researching the past,' Morris explained proudly. 'They're hoping to find out more about the Romans who once lived here. It's interesting wondering what happened a long time ago.'

This information seemed to make Roderick more agitated, not less, so Morris decided it was time they went. He turned to Flick. But she was running after something. 'Flick, stop! It's dangerous that way,' he shouted in alarm, seeing his cousin racing away with her hands out.

'She's so stupid,' he told Roderick, wishing Flick would stop fooling around and come back. 'My father says she's totally incapable of staying still. She's probably trying to catch a dragonfly... Did you know that dragonflies were called Horse-Stingers? They were often seen flying round horses in fields. If one of them bit the horse, it made it twitch and skip about like Flick does. People thought the horse had been stung by a dragon, rather than a tiny fly. But I don't think dragonflies come this high uPPP— FLICK!'

Morris's heart lurched as he dashed forward to where his cousin had suddenly disappeared. How far had she slipped? Was she hurt? How would he get help to pull her up?

But Roderick was suddenly in front of him at the edge.

'It's okay. Don't worry! Your cousin is safe. It's just a slip onto a little bit of rock…a ledge, you might say.'

Morris tried to push past Roderick but the man placed a hand on his shoulder. 'No, stay back. The rubble is slippery near the edge. Your friend's eyes are shut – probably a bit dazed. But I think I can reach her.'

'What if you slip, too? What shall I do?' Morris's heart was thudding like the drum of an aeroplane engine.

'I'll be careful. I'm heavier than you so I won't slip. Be taking your pullover off. We'll make it into a pillow to cushion her head while she recovers.'

Morris didn't like taking orders from a stranger – he wasn't sure yet that he could trust this one. But he also knew he had no choice. He couldn't pull Flick up alone. And he didn't want to annoy the man. He might still go down and tell his parents about the stone throwing.

So he yanked his pullover up over his head. And then froze, arms in the air, pullover round his elbows.

There was a dragon in front of him. One second, Roderick had been about to climb down, the next second a dragon was hovering on the edge of the steep drop to the field below, silhouetted against the sun, scales glistening and wings stretched wide.

For an instant, his gold-green eyes peered straight at Morris – and then Roderick was standing over Flick, looking concerned.

'She's a little concussed,' the man said. 'But I think she's not badly hurt. Give me your pullover.'

'But—' Morris started. Then stopped.

Surely he'd imagined it? He'd desperately wanted something to rescue Flick and his imagination had supplied it. But no! He hadn't been wishing anything. He'd definitely seen a dragon.

'I thought I saw...' His voice trailed off. He felt shaky, as if he'd missed breakfast.

Roderick was watching him with a strange look on his face. 'Fear makes our brains do all sorts of things,' he said. 'Look, she's coming round now.'

Flick sat up slowly and said, 'Sorry. I slipped. Thanks for pulling me up – I presume that's what you did?'

'It was nothing,' said Roderick, gruffly. 'You'll be all right now. But I hope you've learned your lesson.'

'I have,' said Flick fervently, rubbing her leg and straightening her shirt and pullover, which now had little pieces of grass and soil all over.

Morris bit back a comment about how disgustingly grubby she looked, and realised he was simply glad she was safe. He turned instead to their rescuer. 'Look, Roderick, we don't know you very well, but we're sorry about the stone and really grateful you helped

Flick just now. Come and see the dig if you want. Dad won't mind, so long as you're interested in old things.'

Roderick nodded, but seemed keen to get off. 'Thank you, thank you,' he murmured as he waved goodbye. They watched as he went on his way. Morris thought he walked rather slowly and carefully. Maybe he was older than he looked and tired after a climb in the sun.

They tramped equally slowly back to camp. For once, Flick didn't run ahead or shout and play around. Morris was relieved because he didn't feel like talking. His brain was jumping around like a firecracker as first one thought then another exploded inside him. He needed to think calmly. The man had been helpful but there was something odd about him. There was definitely a connection between this stranger and the dragon that he thought – he knew – he'd seen. But people just didn't turn into dragons. So he must have imagined it. He sighed, wishing his heartbeat would slow down. Perhaps Roderick was merely one of those circus magicians who visited the area in summer.

He noticed that Flick was scuffing the soles of her shoes at every step. He said at one point, 'You'll cop it if you wear them out, Flick.' But even as he tried to concentrate on how cross his aunt would be when she saw the damage, his thoughts kept returning to his worry. And why was that pottery shard he'd found the other day suddenly jumping about in his mind along with all the other thoughts? Was he going mad?

He walked on, chewing his lip, still trying to settle his pounding heart by breathing as slowly as he could

– which was difficult while walking. They were nearly down the hill when the first line of tents came into sight. He could make out the grownups bent over the earthworks, oblivious to everything around them. They hadn't wanted Morris's pottery shard. Said it was irrelevant. But something had attracted him to it and made him stow it safely in an old hanky in the canvas pocket on his tent wall. It was a mottled orangey-cream colour with a little scratching on its surface. The sort of mark made in the surface by a sharp instrument. He'd only noticed it when he was washing it in the plastic sink they used to clean up all the finds.

Now he thought about it, the marking looked just like the arrowed point of a dragon tail. In fact, just like the tail of the dragon he'd seen when he took his pullover off…

That was it! His subconscious had been proving to him something he already knew. He knew he'd seen a dragon and his memory was trying to make him admit it. His heart raced even faster. If he'd imagined the dragon, the dragon wouldn't have had reason to look at him with those fierce gold-green eyes. And if he hadn't imagined it, the dragon had indeed looked at him and knew he'd been seen. He glanced behind him, half fearful of finding those huge webbed wings bearing down on him with a snort of fiery-red dragonbreath.

CHAPTER 5

The Shard

*B*ack at Musselburgh, Scordril wasted no time in assembling the council again. He'd rejoined Ygdrann at the place where they had parted earlier and his thoughts were taking shape in his mind even as they flew back to their own layr. But he made Ygdrann wait for news until they were once more in the Great Hall. Ygdrann wasn't happy and snorted his disagreement. But Scordril needed to tell the council of the things he'd seen and tasted, and it would be easiest to tell all the mages at the same time. Besides, Androtta was needed to record what Scordril had to say.

The council reformed quickly. The other dragons sat as they had that morning but Scordril stood next to the fire. His eyes flashed with the reflections from the firelight. He was too agitated to sit, and paced as he spoke.

»*The magic barrier exists! It is there just as Gylning said. And it encircles the layr, as far as I could tell, in the manner the Chronicles suggest. I tasted very strong magic. Ancient mixed with more modern. If the spell was struck by the nightdragons, then since the Chronicles suggested that they had no magics, the* nightdragons must have got magic from elsewhere. The Chronicles record that some Traprain dragons wondered if it might be connected with the harness the nightdragons tried to steal, or if the smallone Brekk might have had undiscovered mage power.»

Scordril stopped and looked at each of the council members in turn. »I venture that the smallone had that power and the nightdragons have somehow used it to fashion this wicked magic.»

They were silent until Kvayn spoke. »Yes, of course...The nightdragons wanted the ancient harness. If they got access to some other item like that, it could have been mixed with the bones or skin of the smallone to make this powerful magic. Cast and set near Traprain, and maturing with time!»

The others all spoke at once. But Scordril's mindlink was strongest.

»The missing portion of the harness...The piece that was never found.» Scordril felt as if thousands of ants were crawling up his tail as he spoke. »That is what they used, it has to be!»

»How, in a million sun-rounds can we find an antidote to that?» Ygdrann's voice squealed as if he had stepped on a sharp stone.

»It will take the combined minds of many dragons to solve this.» Kvayn's voice rumbled around the Hall. »So, Scordril, could you sense dragonkin?»

»No...I was morphed as an overgrounder most of the time, but my dragonsenses should still have worked. It seems the magic is so strong it makes any mindlink near impossible. I doubt I could even have called for *help… Foolishly I did not think to try.*» Scordril barely paused, breathing deeply before he delivered the worst news. *»AND I found that there are overgrounders right over the layr. They are archaeologists on a 'dig'.*»

Scordril paused to see if any of the others knew what that was. He sensed confusion. So he explained what he had seen. And his unexpected meeting with the two overgrounder children, which had given him an opportunity to ask about the dig. Even having to call himself Roderick to avoid suspicion. He sensed wry amusement at that from the other dragons. He told them everything he could think of, but kept a mental wall round Flick's accident and the fact that Morris had seen him morph briefly to dragon form. Scordril felt guilty about withholding even part of the truth. It felt like a huge weight hanging around his neck and banging against his stomach.

The others shuffled and glanced at each other as they absorbed his words. But Scordril knew what they had to do.

»We must stop this 'dig' before the overgrounders find any relics that might be used to wield power over dragonkind in the future…like the wingriders are trying to now.»

»And we must be quick. What if these diggers find artefacts with dragon icons on them?» Ygdrann's eyes flashed with red lights as he spoke.

»It is also necessary if we are to rescue the dragons at Traprain. We would find it hard otherwise.» Kvayn replied.

»Yes, yes, but are we to rescue the Traprain

dragons?» Fenror cut in rudely, as if he wasn't entirely in favour. He might be impolite but he didn't sound as angry as he had done before, Scordril noted, wondering if Kvayn had spoken with Fenror.

»*We must,*» said Scordril. »*Their fate is ours. If the magic barrier is real then we should assume that nightdragons are real! And if the barrier appeared soon after they did…*»

Scordril felt his tone rising. His fears were engulfing him and he stood still, except for his chocolate-veined wings. He raised them upwards, spreading them wide. He let the firelight sparkle on his bronze scales. Then he let all the anger and despair that had built up inside rush out. All the terrible things behind the words of the Chronicles sprang up like nightmares.

»*Do we wait for the enemy dragons to return? What if they didn't want treasure, but wanted dragonslaves instead? Do we let them take our kin? What if there are no dragons to find, because we let them die? We are next! They will burn, torture and kill… Or maybe the overgrounders will steal our magic first? To trap us for themselves.*» Scordril's eyes were wide, flashing gold and green. He shook with a mixture of rage and terror. His dread was reflected in the faces of the council. Each mask-like face as horrified as the next. »*Either way we are doomed.*»

»*Scordril is right.*» Kvayn said calmly, soothing the minds of the others like the dragonmaster she was. Scordril's anger receded as he sensed her mind was made up and she would lead the dragons into action. »*And the overgrounders must be stopped. We cannot allow them to see our rescue or find any discarded, unthought-of bits of ancient dragon artefacts. In those may lie the power of the barrier. And of the antidote.»*

»But how to stop them?» Ygdrann turned his head to look at each council member in turn.

»Tomorrow, after the overgrounders rising time, I will call again upon the youngones I met there. One of them – the male – appeared trustworthy. At least I can find out more before we act. Perhaps I myself can dig and find a relic to use in countering the magic barrier.» Scordril knew that sounded more like a hope than a real possibility. *»The existence of Lothian dragonkind is at stake!»*

—◦◦◦—

Morris was up before Flick, even though Flick had disturbed him with her torchlight for ages and he'd then had to endure the sounds of her fidgeting around next door to get comfortable in her sleeping bag before she finally fell asleep. Morris had taken ages to nod off after that and felt like he'd barely slept at all. His mind had worked until the early hours on the puzzle of whether Roderick could possibly have changed into a dragon, or a dragon could possibly have changed into Roderick.

Still in his pyjamas, with a jumper over them, he knelt just inside the tent opening and poked his head out to stare at the early morning dew, twinkling in the rising sun. He'd found his shard while helping with the dig three days before. A shard with a peculiar etching on it that reminded him of a dragon's tail. A tail like the one the Roderick/dragon figure had sported. He ran his hand through the damp grass, feeling the dew trickle between his fingers, and thought. What if a dragon-man had appeared and rescued Flick? A bit like one of the daring tales in her Beano Books. But no. As he wiped his hand on his jumper, Morris reminded himself that that only happened in stories.

Flick woke up and emerged bleary-eyed from her tent. Together, they rekindled the remains of last night's fire, blowing it into existence with a cloud of black, sooty smoke, and put some eggs into the billycan to boil.

Morris ate with a frown on his face.

'You okay, or what?' Flick wiped some egg from around her mouth. 'I won't go home if you don't want.'

Morris shook his head. 'I'm fine, just a bit tired. Bit hard to sleep with that glaring searchlight bouncing around all night!' He looked sternly at her and Flick flushed. Then he laughed. 'No need to stick around on my account. And I know how keen you are to get some better shoes. You could, of course, not kick them around like a donkey.'

Flick threw a punch at him, ducked her head just in case, then asked, 'What will you do while I'm gone?'

'Help Mum and Dad and the others.'

But Flick had stopped listening. A car rumbled and jolted across the field. She jumped up. 'My lift into the village. Your turn to wash up again! Make sure you do it properly.' With a grin, she climbed in and waved to Morris as she was driven away.

Morris, for once, was grateful to be alone, despite

the greasy plates and spoons. He wanted to help his parents and their team. *It'll give me time to think and ask some questions,* he told himself. *They're all interested in history. Maybe I can find out if there were ever such things as man-dragons. But if so, why would one be on Traprain Law in the school holidays. I bet it's not for walking.*

Morris decided to help Grace. She was one of the 'washers' responsible for cleaning up broken pottery and bones and things found on the dig. Her tables and water trough were set up behind one of the larger tents and he watched as she gently swilled some pieces in a dish of water to see them more clearly. The items appeared and disappeared under the swirling water. She carefully whisked away the last traces of soil, using a small wooden-handled brush, then lifted the pieces from the shallow water to spread them out on a table in the shade, below a damp cloth. He was soon busy with some small pieces of pottery that he was allowed to clean. While they worked, he tried asking her about the history of the place in ancient times, but, disappointingly, she seemed uninterested in anything beyond taking care of the finds. 'That's for others who know more than me,' was all she would say. And with that he had to be content, though his mind was still agitated.

When he looked up later, Morris's heart started pounding so much he nearly dropped the piece of pot he was holding: Roderick was standing by the corner of the farthest tent. One of the male archaeologists was with him – Morris could hear their laughter and voices, half drowned out by the sound of Grace pouring away some water. He couldn't believe his luck: perhaps he could find out more about the stranger. He started to put the pottery down.

But at that moment, the archaeologist pointed over to Morris and walked away. Roderick strode over the trampled grass towards him. He looked just the same as yesterday, with the same clothes and stick, as he called, 'Hello, I've been looking for you. I took up your invitation to visit.' He waited while Morris wiped his hands dry and apologised to Grace for having to go so soon.

'How's the head, sir?' Morris asked, suddenly worried in case Roderick wasn't as pleased as he looked.

'Fine... Morris, isn't it? But please, it is all right if you call me Roderick. And how is your cousin?' Roderick sounded genuinely concerned about Flick.

'Fully recovered. But she's had to go to the village. Her parents own the shop there. Did you come to see her?'

'Yes and no... I'm glad she's fine, of course, but I thought it would be fun to come and find out more about the dig while I'm in the area. Will you show me around?'

'Of course. I'll check with Dad... You can meet him, and Mum too. Just don't mention Roman spoons or he'll go on till the cows come home,' Morris added, grinning mischievously.

Morris's dad was more than happy to have an interested visitor, and the rest of the morning disappeared while Roderick was shown from one stage of the dig to the next by the various members of the team. He seemed particularly interested in the things that had been found. Morris's mother showed him a few items she was labelling. *I wonder if he's a treasure hunter, or even a thief?* Morris thought nervously. He'd be in a whole heap of trouble if he were. He reminded himself that dragons in stories used to have piles of treasure. But that was silly; that was in fairytales not in real life. If Roderick was a dragon in disguise as a person – or was that a person in disguise as a dragon? – he wouldn't be here looking at things and asking questions, would he? No, Morris reasoned, he'd just breathe fire and trample the diggers into the ground and take whatever dragons take. Besides, he might be from outer space, not a dragon at all... He'd thought about that, too, in the middle of the night. With a shock, he realised that his mother was speaking to him.

'Why don't you take our visitor around to the canteen tent and get some lunch for yourselves?' She wiped her hands on her overalls and smiled pleasantly at them both. 'I'm sure he's had enough of our work for now. And it'll be a nice change for you not to cook on sticks and twigs, for once.'

Roderick stuck close to Morris and seemed amazed at the selection of food. 'Not bad is it, considering? What would you like?' Morris passed a metal plate to Roderick. 'There's salad... and hard-boiled eggs there... or you could have meat pie – it'll be last night's of course...'

Roderick said nothing as Morris pointed and he only

75

took a sliver of the meat pie. He obviously wasn't hungry.

Morris pointed to a place in the shade of one of the tents. 'Let's sit over here and get out of this disgusting sun.' They settled down cross-legged on the grass to eat. Roderick quickly polished off his small piece of pie, but neither said much until Morris sat back and rubbed his stomach.

'Will your cousin be back soon?' Roderick asked, swatting a fly away from his empty plate.

'Later,' said Morris absently, his mind by now on something very different.

He wanted to show Roderick the shard of pottery with the 'tail' etching, and ask him about it, but that meant running over to their tents. He turned to Roderick. 'Look, I've got a piece of something I found that I'd like you to see… It's not valuable,' he added hurriedly, as Roderick's eyes glinted brightly. 'It's just er…very interesting. I'm sure you'll think so too. My tent is over there. Would you come with me, please?'

Roderick seemed pleased to go with him. Morris left him outside their two tents, staring back at the dig, while he went in to fetch the shard. It was dim and cool inside, but he quickly slipped his hand into the pocket on the tent wall where he'd hidden the palm-sized piece of pottery, then clambered out of the tent and held the orangey-cream shard up to Roderick.

Morris watched Roderick's face carefully to see his reaction. He seemed transfixed by the drawing etched into the piece of pot. Morris turned the shard towards the sun where its surface took on an ethereal glow. He kept a firm hold on it as Roderick reached out to touch it. The man seemed to flinch as his long bony finger made contact with it.

⸺◦◦◦⸺

Scordril felt the painful twinge of ancient magic through his fingertips. It stung them like nettles. A rainbow of colours showered the air before his eyes and excitement filled him. Even morphed as Roderick, Scordril knew that this was the same magic he'd tasted in the barrier around Traprain Law. This might be what he needed, what he'd told the other dragons he would try to find when he returned to Traprain.

Fear swallowed his initial excitement. If this artefact had been found, how many others lay awaiting discovery? The archaeologists would surely find some more while they dug. Or they might have picked some up already. Pots with etchings were old and special, and they were obviously imbued with ancient magic because of the uses they'd been put to.

Scordril forgot where he was for a moment as he pondered what the ancients might have used the special pots for. He himself had never seen one, though he'd heard of them. If he ever got into Traprain Law, that was something he'd like to ask.

With a start, he realised that Morris was staring up at him with a look of concern. And an idea flashed across Scordril's mind. *It'll mean getting overgrounder Morris to co-operate,* he reasoned. *It'll be a risk.* But Morris seemed the sort of overgrounder to keep a secret. And after all, Scordril argued to himself, he was sure Morris had seen him morph back to human form so there was nothing much else to lose. The dragons in general were against deliberate contact between dragon and human ever since the Split, but there were no firm rules and there was something about the boy that he found invited trust, an affinity with things that could not always be seen. Hadn't he told him about the legends of the dragonfly? But the cousin who couldn't keep still – she mustn't know. She took risks without thinking, like running too close to the edge of the Law, and she seemed as if she would happily talk to every overgrounder within earshot. No, she definitely mustn't know. But Morris could be very useful.

Scordril let his overgrounder face relax into a smile.

'That is very interesting, Morris,' he said, withdrawing his fingers. 'It has reminded me of something I came to tell you. The real reason I came back to the dig. A secret you may have guessed already. Can we talk?' Scordril watched Morris, as several emotions seemed to fight for supremacy on the boy's face. Morris first frowned, then his lips twitched into a nervous smile and he gripped the shard between both hands.

'Yes, sir… Roderick. And I have some questions to ask you. May I?' The boy's face looked eagerly up at him. Scordril was now certain that his idea stood a good chance of working.

'Of course. Can we sit down? Somewhere where we can see when Flick returns?'

They settled themselves with their backs towards the guy ropes and the drainage ditch that was dug on the north-eastern side of the tent, facing out over the grass towards the dig.

'We'll see Flick from here, easily. And we can't be overheard.' Morris bent his knees up, lent forward and placed the piece of orangey-cream pottery between his feet. 'You first.'

Scordril smiled at the polite instruction. 'Well, I'm sure you think Flick's rescue was odd, don't you?' He turned towards Morris, hunting the boy's face for some recognition.

'Yup. I mean I know what I think I saw. Rather I know what I saw...' Morris pursed his lips and folded his arms across his bent knees. 'Is your name really Roderick? Do you have a dragon that only comes out when you want it to? I mean, it was a dragon thing that rescued Flick, wasn't it? It wasn't there before and then it was... and you seemed to have vanished...'

Scordril took a deep breath, nodding his dark head as Morris seemed to falter. 'No, my name isn't Roderick. Yes, it was a dragon thing that rescued your cousin and I did vanish. But it's not a dragon thing that comes to me, Morris. It is me. I am a dragon.'

Morris's eyes grew wide and round and his mouth made an 'O' shape but only a whistling sound escaped. Scordril pressed on, his heart pounding with the risk he was taking. 'My proper name is Scordril. I can change myself into overgrounder...I mean human form. Roderick is what I look like when I do. And you saw what I look like when I'm a dragon, didn't you?'

Morris suddenly grinned from ear to ear, as if with pride. 'Yes, I did! Boy! I knew that I'd seen a dragon. Flick didn't, did she? Am I the only person to see one, ever? Well, since the days when knights did?' He looked hopefully back at Scordril.

'Well, you're certainly the first to have seen a dragon for a long time.' Sensing Morris's disappointment, he quickly added, 'And definitely the first to see me morph!'

Morris hugged his knees to his chest and turned his head to gaze towards the dig, as if going into a trance, then back to Scordril, nodding slowly. 'I always wondered if dragons were real. I thought they might be. No smoke without fire, my father would say. And I'm glad it was just me who saw. I won't tell anyone about you, Scorrr..drrill… Flick certainly mustn't know. SHE wouldn't believe in you. She's much too matter of fact. And anyway she's not good at secrets. She might blab all over the place.'

'Thank you. That is what I hoped you'd say. And because you understand, we can be friends and I will trust you with the rest of my secret.' Scordril watched as Morris swallowed hard. He was unsure how much the boy could take in all at once. Or whether he was treating him too much like a youngone. But he needn't have worried.

'The reason why you're here at Traprain Law?' Morris asked in a sensible tone.

'Yes, the reason. You see, there are lots of dragons, some under Musselburgh where I am from—'

Morris appeared to choke before he exclaimed, 'But I'm from there, too. You mean there are real dragons in Musselburgh?'

Scordril laughed and briefly explained about a hidden place excavated off the old mines, near the sewers, where dragons could live unseen. Morris paid rapt attention. 'But that is by the by, Morris. Dragons also live here underneath Traprain Law, except they are now trapped and in grave danger.' Scordril felt the weight of his responsibility as he spoke. 'They are all prisoners of an ancient magic, which locks them into their layr – that's the name we give the place where dragons live underground. I am here to help them escape.'

'Trapped?' Morris's face looked serious. 'Under the ground in a... a... burrow thing? Because of MAGIC?'

Scordril raised a hand as if to calm Morris. 'Well... it's not a burrow, it's a network of tunnels through the rock. And dragons do use magic, you know. This is... is a spell that's been here a long time, that's been growing...'

'...till it's too big? Out of control?' Morris shook his head as if marvelling at the things he was hearing.

Scordril was relieved Morris seemed to be arriving at an answer he could believe. 'Exactly, out of control. We call it a dragongrid. A spell which acts like a barrier, so big and strong that dragons cannot get through from one side to the other.'

'But how will you get in to help, then?' Morris shifted to sit cross-legged with his arms folded like a Red Indian chief. 'Can you magic away the barrier, or make a powerful spell that opens it up.'

'I can't get inside the layr's entrances, as they're sealed by the magic, but yes, I can get inside the grid when I'm Roderick. But I have to be a dragon to help

81

the others escape: I need to create a spell that will remove the barrier, you see.' Scordril eyed the shard now lying where Morris had left it. 'To do that, I need a piece of something with the right sort of magic in it. Like that shard of yours.'

Morris seemed to stop breathing before lunging forward to snatch up the shard. 'You mean that this has magic in it? Dragon magic?'

Scordril wondered fleetingly if it had been a mistake to take Morris into his confidence. He explained carefully that there was magic in the pottery fragment, but that humans would not know. And that, as a dragon, he could try to use that magic to rescue the trapped dragons. Morris sat staring at the shard in his hand as he listened.

'So, you see Morris, if I could borrow that piece of ancient pottery I could rescue the other dragons. It will have to be at night so that we are not seen by overgrounders, but we will find a way. My dragonkin in Musselburgh are waiting, too. They will help. We fear the dragons under Traprain Law may have insufficient water, no food… maybe soon they will even have no air.'

Scordril knew he might be exaggerating but he needed an answer fast. Morris's cousin might come back at any time and the conversation would have to stop. Besides, he was again tiring from staying morphed so long. 'I would return it to you. And I would – will – give you a special dragon gift as a reward for your help.'

Perhaps a talisman, something small with dragonmagic in it that would help protect Morris from danger, he thought. He would decide what the gift would be when the shard's magic had been used and the Traprain dragons rescued. He paused, waiting for Morris's reply.

The boy was turning the shard over and over in his hands, as if thinking carefully. Then he looked up and met Scordril's stare. 'You can borrow the shard if it will help the others. But how will I get it back? I'd like to keep it.'

Scordril stood up and inclined his head, without answering immediately. 'Thank you,' he said.

Morris rose, too, perhaps recognising the solemn nature of the decision he'd just made. Scordril stretched out his hand for the shard, sensing that Morris seemed to hesitate before letting him take it.

Scordril gripped it in his right fist as if it would fly away, wincing as the surge of magic rippled across his skin. Reaching out, he placed his other hand on Morris's shoulder. 'Trust me, Morris. I'll find you...soon.'

CHAPTER 6

The Spell

Scordril flapped his wings gently and hovered for the kill. The green sunny expanse of Lothian was laid out under him like a miniature world. Knowing what awaited him back at the layr, he would prefer to stay hung in the air forever.

He turned his head to glance over at Threah, pleased to note that she was poised motionless five wingspans away. He enjoyed hunting expeditions when she accompanied him. The rest of the dragons were away to the south. They were careful to hunt over a large area. Too many dragon 'clouds' causing shadows to chase across the meadows against the natural laws of wind movement would certainly alert the herds of sheep and cows to an imminent dragonraid.

»*Why would I ever hunt alone when I can have you as companion?*« he said gently into her mind. Threah had always been beautiful to him, with her sleek, blue-grey scales and those pale golden eyes that looked on him with approval – but she also teased him mercilessly when she chose to play hard to get. He would become a bonded pair with her one day, that much he knew – just as he knew they would feast well today. The overground animals were stretched out dozing as the heat grew in intensity towards mid-glow. Soon it would become unbearable.

»*One each now and one for later?*« came the amused voice in his mind, as if she had read his thoughts, despite his attempt at shielding.

They dived in unison, their wings barely a span apart now. The two sheep were dead instantly and Scordril and Threah tore greedily at the meat with their teeth and claws, neither of them wasting time in talk.

No overgrounder was anywhere to be seen so there was no need to spare energy for maintaining an illusory cover. Scordril was quite disappointed about this because both he and Threah enjoyed competing with one another to 'create' the best trees and bushes. All dragons chose these in preference to white fluffy clouds when they were on the ground during a hunt, not only because it was more fun but also because clouds on the ground would have drawn more attention than even a full-grown dragon! But shrubbery took more energy from the mages who channelled the magic, so they chose wisely at all times. Scordril, of course, generated his own mage energy and fed some to Threah too.

Now, a fair breeze cooled their hides and Scordril relaxed onto his haunches to take stock of his plan. Threah continued chomping at her beast – as always, he observed with amusement, she was trying to get every last scrap of meat off it.

»*We're taking another two with us. Or have you forgotten?*«

»*I'm hungry. I've been working harder since*

Gylning arrived. My second beast will be a heifer full of blood iron to strengthen him while he heals.»

»*Hmm…*» said Scordril thoughtfully, and rumbled his throat meaningfully.

»*You always rumble like a monster when something is bothering you, Scordril. You sound more like a threatening storm than a friend.*»

»I'm *not the threat,*» Scordril roared, rising up instantly and flicking his tail with a terrifying swish of air that moved the grass he stood on. »*It's that dragongrid, by my claws!*» His temper pushed up to his throat, which rumbled again, even more alarmingly. His wings tensed.

Threah angled her snout menacingly in front of his.

»*Scordril! That anger is a disgrace to you as a mage. Speak out what you feel and be done with the drama. How can we find a future together if you make me afraid?*»

Scordril stared at her, feeling her displeasure, and knowing his gold-green eyes were whirring with an excitement he didn't want her to see. So she was interested in him!

»*I apologise,*» he said, lowering his snout, the anger leaving him as suddenly as it came. »*But the mages are meeting within a glow-mark from now. I am not sure how the experiment will go. Fenror will be insufferable if I fail. I think he would be pleased not to have to help Traprain Law.*»

»*Maybe so. And perhaps you* will *fail first time. The shard is the answer, but who can know how it should be used? You will have to find a way by failure and trial.*»

The sense of her words pleased him but did little to

relieve his growing worry as they hastily killed two heifers and carried them back to the layr. The planned experiment he had dreamed up in the night was going to stretch his powers to their limit and he had no idea if they would even survive the magic that would be created.

⸻⟨⊙⟩⟨⊙⟩⸻

Kvayn called the assembled mages to order.

The cave at the side of the Great Hall was darker than Scordril had remembered. But, being small and rounded, the room was perfect for the experiment he planned to conduct.

The walls here backed on to solid rock rather than other tunnels and rooms. Where it adjoined the Great Hall, the skilled dragondiggers who extended the layr out from the mine workings had thought it best to leave the supporting rock wall thick so that the Hall would not be in danger of collapse if the overgrounders built directly above.

Scordril glanced round the now quietened group, catching each dragon's eyes and sending an image of concentrated magework. The amount of whirring in green and red that he saw in those eyes worried him: the other mages had less idea of what they were doing than he had – and he himself was worried enough for all dragonkin.

A familiar voice broke into his thoughts.

»*So a clump of grass and a piece of pottery is to save*

dragonkind?» Fenror asked, his tone tinged with sarcasm. *»It will add a certain interest to the Chronicles for our offspring, for sure.»*

Scordril sighed. He had wondered about hiding the grass mound until he had explained. Fenror was so influenced by his father's prejudices that he couldn't see beyond the sheepskin to the meat.

»If you touch that clump of grass, as you call it, you will see why it is here.»

Fenror stumped forward and reached out with his claw. At the last minute, he turned his snout to Scordril. *»This is a trick,»* he said. *»I shall not fall for it.»* And he stumped backwards, rather ungracefully, to his place, without touching the grass.

Scordril allowed his jaw to relax a fraction. *»Good,»* he said. *»Because my arm was strangely paralysed for half the hours of darkness after carrying it home last glow. It is a tiny part of the dragongrid.»*

A snort of alarm echoed violently round the chamber at this news. Kvayn and Ygdrann reared and moved further away. Fenror stood subdued, watching. Well, at least he had their attention now. To Scordril's amusement, Androtta simply carried on writing as Scordril indicated the grassy fragment of dragongrid.

»How else are we to test the magic we make?»

Kvayn spoke up at last. *»We have no time to lose, Scordril. Please explain to us what we must do. You said you wanted to work in here so that any rogue magic can be contained. That at least sounds a good idea.»*

Scordril took Morris's shard from where it lay on

the floor beside him and, holding it carefully between two claws, moved it to the centre of the room. The room was not large by dragon standards and he knew that they would all immediately see the etching of the dragon tail on its orangey-cream surface.

»*I can feel the ancient magic in this shard. Touch it and see for yourselves that it was made by the ancestors. This belongs to the young overgrounder, Morris, who I told you about. I probed his mind while we ate lunch yesterday and I swear to you his loyalty. We may yet have need of his help again. I will return the shard to him when we have used it.*»

»*He is a risk, I say,*» said Fenror, rising off his haunches.

»*It is all a risk,*» said Kvayn quietly. »*The overgrounder is a risk. The mixing of magic is a risk. We are risking our lives because we know it is right.*»

Scordril suddenly remembered the hunting flight he had enjoyed with Threah. »*If we don't take the risk, the Traprain Law dragons will never again ride the airwaves or dive on their prey. They will never circle in courtmaking rituals or tend their youngones. Without our help they will perish. So we will start. And we will work together. Otherwise we will all perish because someone failed to play their part.*» He stared directly into Fenror's grey-green darting eyes, which were always on the lookout for a problem, always suspicious. His purple-grey hide was covered in a glistening sheen. Perhaps fear drove his arguments. »*We need your skill, Fenror,*» he said simply.

»I will do as you request,» the older mage said, bowing his head. *»I do not like it but I will not let us down.»*

⸺◦◦◦⸺

Scordril placed the sheepskin bowl of water in the centre of the room. He watched it for a long moment until the waves stopped moving and he could see his reflection clearly. By dragonclaws! His snout was pale and lined with stress. He'd be lucky to reach two hundred sunrounds this way, never mind have a youngone.

He stood up awkwardly. He had not been kidding about the paralysis brought on by carrying the grassy clump home. His whole body from wingtip to footclaw had felt its effect.

He turned slowly to face his fellow mages, ranged in a half circle behind him. The looks of sympathy he read in their swirling eyes touched him. They had obviously read his thoughts.

»Kvayn will seal the bowl,» he said. *»She has skill with containing spells. The water, too, will help hold things together like the bandage on Gylning's wing. It is the best we can do to safeguard the layr.»*

The male dragons watched silently as Kvayn seemed to freeze, as if she had left her body to fetch the spell she needed. But they knew from their own experience that she was deep in her mind weaving two strands of magic together, fetching them from within her own energy stream and lacing them together as she applied them to the bowl on the stone floor.

»*There!*» breathed Ygdrann, visibly relaxing as thin traces of yellow and green shimmered along the edges of the bowl, slid down the sides in a cascade of light and held still for a moment before fading to nothing, leaving a very ordinary-looking skin bowl. »*I always feel better when we get started. I hate all the waiting.*»

Scordril moved forward, Morris's shard in his hand. He broke a small lump off the end and put the rest down beside him. Then he lowered the piece carefully into the water, unwilling to disturb the surface more than necessary. Detail, he told himself. Attention to detail will be what counts.

»*I have taken only a small piece because we must be careful using the ancient magic stored in it. We will proceed as discussed this morning. When we channel some of our own mage power into the shard, it will mix with the ancient magic and begin to form something else – something like the strange power that is holding the dragongrid in place. But our own magic may be slightly different from that of the smallone Brekk whose power – if we suspect correctly – was in its infancy. So we must try it out slowly and carefully and adjust it to match the barrier's magic.*»

The mages nodded briefly in acknowledgement and stilled themselves. Scordril, too, sank to his haunches, and focused inwards until he came to that place where he had built the shield that protected his mind from too much incoming data and from too many dragons reading his thoughts.

He lowered the shield and then felt the other mages link in turn into his mind. First, Ygdrann slid into place, a calm, friendly presence that immediately eased Scordril's tension and restored some of the strength he had used on his day out with Morris at Traprain Law and in bringing the fragment of dragongrid home. Then Kvayn linked in, decisive in her hold, and finally Fenror. Scordril was surprised and also relieved to find the mage focused and purposeful, rather than reluctant. He was clearly keeping his pledge to help, not hinder.

When the link was firmly established, Scordril sent the signal to start to each of them, and a stream of mage power began to enter his mind. Small at first, then growing in power as the mages grew more confident. He gathered it for a split second and then very gently sent it onwards to the shard in the bowl. He did not add his own. He would not be joining them in making the new spell. He had another role for himself. But he needed to monitor their mixing because he was the only one who had direct experience of the barrier. Right now, he concentrated on channelling the power to the inside of the shard, sitting at the bottom of the bowl of water.

A hum began to resonate around the thick rock of the walls. The fragment broken from Morris's pottery changed from its deep orangey-cream colour and took on a reddish brown shade, as if filling up with handfuls of earth that were pushing to escape. The hum increased in intensity and Scordril's scales tingled under the effect. The magic residing in the shard began to change in nature, turning from something they were familiar with from their ancestors' artefacts, to something that jolted and jerked away from their sensing, as if fighting to avoid joining with their own more modern mage power. The energy finally built up inside the shard and coalesced into a force so strong that their mindlink vibrated painfully. Scordril withstood this initial onslaught and held onto the mage link. Then he, too, found himself struggling. The hum reached a crescendo and the headpain increased. Shocked, he willed them to taste the strange magic they had made and know it for themselves.

A surge too far, and an explosion of brown energy and light erupted from the shard, causing the water in the bowl to hiss and bubble. The shock forced their mindlink apart as if a locked door had suddenly opened as they pulled on it, and the mages collapsed, their minds overcome with headpain.

Fenror was first to regain his senses. »*Perhaps we should fill the room with water and grow gills,*« he said drily. »*I, for one, would feel safer. You look er... nervous, Scordril.*«

»*Me? Nervous? The sun will surely rise in the west tomorrow!*« He flapped his wings humorously to laugh off the very idea. But underneath, he knew they were all shocked at the power of the raw and strange energy they had created in the shard – and sobered at the thought that they had pushed it a snout too far.

»*At least we know where to stop,*« observed Kvayn quietly, shaking her neck around as if to clear her head. »*Are we to taste the energy and check if it matches the dragongrid magic?*«

»*That was the plan,*« said Scordril, straightening himself.

They sniffed round the shard and then the grassy clump, taking turns to assess the match and recall the point at which they had reached a match as they streamed their flows through Scordril.

At that moment, Threah appeared, carrying a bowl. »*Drink this,*« she commanded. »*It is a tincture of feverfew and will quickly take away the headpain. But perhaps you should also take more care – that hum has affected three of our watchdragons and some of the youngones who were nearby.*«

Ygdrann and Kvayn looked somewhat shame-faced at forgetting to warn the other dragons to stay well away. Fenror seemed rather pleased with himself. Scordril took the bowl from Threah gratefully and slurped a large mouthful before handing it to the others, who did the same. When Threah had gone, he said, »*Threah is always just where you need her. I feel better already.*«

»*We need to make a large amount of this energy,*« Kvayn reminded them. »*Exactly at the strength where it matches the dragongrid. Are we going to hurl the energy at the barrier, Scordril?*«

»*I don't think so,*« said Scordril slowly. »*I have been thinking about it since this morning. If we fight like with like, we may create an impasse, a stand-off, as when two dragons practise battle flight manoeuvres but are so equally matched in talent neither can win.*« He banged his clawed fists together to emphasise his point. »*So I thought of something different that will give us a better chance of succeeding.*«

He paused a moment. What if his plan was wrong and he endangered them by trying to be too clever?

»*Tell us your idea,*» said Fenror. »*We are all able to judge for ourselves and be responsible for the decision together.*»

Scordril blinked his eyes at him, thankful for the reasoned response, and straightened. »*I thought that we would use the new energy to launch an attack on me—*»

»*To WHAT?*» Ygdrann thundered. »*Are you taking leave of your dragonsense? If you – single-handedly – were not able to remove the barrier when you visited, strong as you are, how do you think you will withstand us firing such alien magic at you – even if we had enough, which we haven't. It is suicide.*»

Ygdrann, his usual mild approach completely forgotten, stared round at the others for support.

Kvayn stepped forward. »*Scordril is our strongest mage. Let him finish telling us his plan and then we will judge it. You would not, I think, digest the cow before you had eaten it, Fenror?*»

Scordril flapped his wings, more out of frustration than annoyance. »*It is not hard to understand once you hear the plan,*» he said, more confident now he had Kvayn's overt support. »*I will not be contributing to generating or using the alien magic. Instead, I will weave around myself a dense web of fine tendrils of magic, several layers deep. None of the alien power will be able to find a way through. It should invert itself as it meets my resistance and then be deflected onto the dragongrid as a negative image of itself. I think this will cancel out the power in the grid. It will implode and be gone... But I may be wrong. It is a risk, I admit.*»

»*We need to try this out first,*» said Kvayn.

»That is why I brought the grass clump.»

Scordril fetched the clump of grass and placed it in the centre of the room beside the bowl, in which the fragment of pottery was now rocking gently back and forth, a mere dull brown now that they were no longer pushing energy into it. As he noticed this, Scordril reflected ruefully that Morris might not be very pleased at the change in his treasure.

»The room must be protected,» said Kvayn. *»If something goes wrong, the power must be contained here. We cannot risk the layr or the youngones.»* And she immediately went into a trance as she started to weave and then place the containing spell around every part of the walls and room, and across the entrance, though this would not stop anyone leaving. It would, however, contain the magic.

»While Kvayn is doing this for us,» said Scordril quietly, *»perhaps you, Fenror, would fetch a suitably sized rock from the entrance. We will need somewhere to store a large quantity of magic.»*

Several minutes passed, during which Ygdrann and Scordril remained silent. Scordril's mind wondered ahead to the time when they would surely fight the nightdragons. It didn't seem honourable, somehow. They had a despicable life, never able to think for themselves, conditioned to blind obedience – perhaps even as far as remembering to remind the younger generation of their masters to test for the maturing of the spell. He doubted the wingriders would go to such trouble only to leave it in place without coming back. Who would want a layr of dead dragons? Yes, they would surely be returning, and therefore he, Scordril, would have to fight the nightdragons too, if they were to resist this madness.

»*It's not as though we will be breaking the nightdragons' spirits,*» said Ygdrann suddenly, as if he, too, had been thinking the same thoughts. »*They no longer have any honour to compromise. They are machines by now. We can't make an honourable dragon out of dead scales and rotten teeth.*»

Scordril nodded and Ygdrann moved over to allow Fenror to dump the huge rock he had just brought in. Kvayn was looking fully recovered, and the walls and ceiling now retained a glow of yellow and green with a hint of pink flashing among it.

»*I added a silencing spell so that the hum would not reach past the containing spell,*» she explained. »*It is also stronger and therefore more visible.*»

After a short discussion, Scordril watched while the three mages started to make some more magic that exactly matched the alien mixture. The hum was louder, as Kvayn had predicted. They could only hope it was contained. It was not a sound dragon ears could put up with for long – too like the keening of a dragon in distress.

This time, instead of allowing the strange magic to roam free, they channelled it into a corner of the large rock. The water in the sheepskin bowl wobbled but did not hiss.

Scordril knew they would need a short rest after making the required amount so he centred his own thoughts and set about the task of making an intricate web of protecting magic around himself.

He found himself enjoying the exercise. It was rare these days for any of the mages to have to use their power for an unusual project and he took perverse pleasure in weaving the web in blotches of similar and dissimilar colour all over himself, very like the markings on the cattle he killed for food. He wove each of the five patterned layers in the same way the overgrounders made their cloth. He was pleased to note only a very small diminishing of strength as he finished. He was still young, and strong in his mage power.

The others were waiting for him. Fenror spoke. *»If you stand there, Scordril…»* he indicated a place halfway down the longer wall, *»and we stand here…»* he waved Kvayn and Ygdrann to his side, *»I think the angle will be about right for us to send the power we have stored in the rock over to you and for you to send it on to that…that…bit of dragon-disgracing engineered magic.»* He pointed at the grassy clump, his eyes flashing red, and Scordril sensed that he had finally overcome his distrust of the Traprain Law dragons.

Scordril sent a sign to the others and they each bent to their task: the mages to directing the store of energy, Scordril to resisting it as it hit him.

Surprisingly, there was no hum. At first, he found it difficult to redirect the inverting magic and also maintain his shielding. The cave walls became peppered with indentations and sandy lumps fell to the stone floor. This was not how to do it. They did not need a magic that would inscribe the walls of a cave!

He reached into himself for more power – and started tightening the outer layer of the invisible structure woven around himself, so that it became like a fishing net that is stretched to breaking point. This brought instant results.

The inverted alien power hit the grassy clump spot-on and a sheet of screaming white light streaked across the cave. It shut their eyes with pain. Their ears went deaf. The mages bent double under the onslaught.

Scordril alone was unaffected. The protection he'd woven seemed to stop the implosion's shockwaves in its tracks. He suddenly realised that there was complete and utter silence. No one moved.

The green and yellow glow on the cave walls was vibrating. Scordril thought wrily that the preparations he had deemed adequate only a moment earlier now seemed all too thin – but they had held.

After a while, they sent for Threah who brought them more feverfew, this time mixed with sorrel to boost their vitamin C, she told them. »*It seems you are bent on destroying yourselves today,*« she said. »*Perhaps I had better make some more, if this sort of behaviour is to continue.*«

Scordril knew she was joking but the others looked shocked.

»*If we are putting you to any bother...*« Ygdrann began. But Threah dismissed him with a mock roar and waved as she once more left them to work.

»*When we are ready,*« said Scordril soberly, »*we need to fill this rock with alien magic so that it can be transported to the site. We cannot hope to make enough if we do it when we are there. We must knock out the dragongrid in one go or the nightdragons may find out* what we are doing before we are finished. *If they are watching us, of course. They may not be.*»

Fenror looked troubled. »*I believe we must do this,*» he said. »*But just suppose the so-called wingriders have already got to the Traprain Law dragons and are using them to trap us? We would be playing into their hands.*»

»*So why now rather than last sun-round or fifty sun-rounds ago if they wanted to do that?*» said Scordril. »*No, the power has matured and they have captured our kin on purpose. The time is now. The need for courage is now. There is no one but us. We must get on with making the store of dragongrid magic so that we can be done with this aberration before they do decide to use the Traprain Law dragons to turn on us, too.*»

CHAPTER 7

Hairy Craig

'Hello there! Who are you?'

At the sound of Flick's voice, Morris dragged his mind back to the present and away from the uncomfortable rock he was sitting on and his thoughts of Roderick, or rather Scordril, and the things he'd said. He craned forward. But all he could see beyond Flick was a cat – a very big cat. 'That? Where did that come from?'

'Dunno, just appeared… Must've been hiding in the rocks, behind us up there, on the top of Hairy Craig maybe…' She waved her sandwich and beckoned with her other hand. 'Want something to eat, do you?'

Morris watched the interloper lazily. Hairy Craig wasn't too far from the dig; a lump of scraggy stone between Traprain Law and the sea. It made a good place to have a picnic tea away from the adults. From here he could see the surrounding countryside one way or, if he looked the other, Bass Rock, rising from the sea in the distance. But it seemed an unlikely place to find cats.

Nevertheless, the cat was real and seemed to have Flick's full attention. 'Want a piece then?' Flick extracted the ham from the sandwich and threw it down near the cat.

Morris sat up. 'Hey!'

The cat sniffed at the meat and gobbled it up.

Flick pushed the remains of the sandwich into her mouth, and brushed away the tomato juice that dribbled down her chin.

Morris sat staring at the strange animal. It seemed even bigger than he first thought. Its fur was longer than a normal cat's, and covered in an odd patchwork of colours. It was mostly gingery brown, but there were splodges of black, dark brown and cream all jumbled up amongst each other. Tortoiseshell. His grandmother had had one.

Green eyes shifted from Morris to Flick and back again, as the cat seemed to size them up.

There was something slightly spooky about the cat's eyes. 'That thing looks half wild,' Morris said. 'Probably a feral cat.'

'Probably.' Flick brushed the last of her picnic crumbs from her shorts and settled back against the rock. The cat arched itself and hissed, then moved to sit further away and wash its tufted ears.

'That hair makes him look just like your friend Archie Thomson. Remember him?' Flick said.

'Spitting image.'

Flick laughed and clapped her hand on her knee. 'Archie Thomson – AT! That's what we'll call him, Ay-Tee – if it is a "him", that is.'

'AT it is, whatever,' Morris said, deciding he needed to get away from cat topics. 'Which way do you want to go back to the Law? The quick route we came by? Then we can get rid of these rucksacks.'

Flick, who was still watching AT, pursed her lips and seemed to think. 'The short route, I guess. We don't have to go now though, do we? Let's explore Hairy Craig.'

Morris could think of nothing he'd like more, but knew that the afternoon was getting on and they should be heading back to the camp. 'Haven't we done enough exploring? Besides, if you climb around any more in those shoes, you'll have ruined them like the last pair!'

Morris ducked to avoid Flick's apple core. 'Careful! Chucking things got us into trouble the other day. Come on, let's get tidied up.'

Flick shook out the rug while he picked up the flask of juice and cups and stowed them in his rucksack next to his torch and penknife.

'Morris, why don't we come back later? I bet it would be exciting by moonlight. If it's as bright and clear as last night, we could explore.' She paused as they were tying up the rug with a piece of old string and looked at Morris. 'We needn't tell.'

But Morris was thinking... what if Scordril were to come this way tonight, on his way to rescue the other dragons? The last thing he'd want was an audience. Morris knew he'd love to see the dragons himself, find out if the plan worked. *But we can't be here then. I can't let Flick see the dragons. She thinks Scordril is, well, Roderick.*

Flick grabbed him by the arm. Her eyes gleamed. 'Well? We could, couldn't we?'

Morris was struggling to come up with his answer

when a flash of ginger, black and cream darted past his legs, pushed its head into his rucksack and started to paw at the contents. 'Scram!' he yelled.

'Leave him be!' Flick said. 'I thought you liked animals.'

'I do, but… scoot!' AT gave a muffled hiss as Morris tried to drag the bag away. He brandished his fist at the cat.

AT hurled himself at Morris leaving a set of red claw marks down one shin. Livid, Morris pursued the cat. He caught up with the animal as it disappeared into a hole between two rocks.

By the time Flick caught up with him, Morris was staring over a boulder into the hole. There was a sliding noise then a distant yowl.

Flick sounded stricken. 'Is AT trapped down there, do you think?'

Morris's anger evaporated and he felt uneasy. What if AT was trapped and he'd chased him? 'Well AT got in so he can jolly well get out again,' he said, trying not to sound concerned. He fished out his torch and flashed it over the place where the cat had vanished. 'There's a large gap here, going right into the rocks, like a cave…no, wait a minute, it's not that deep. I can see his eyes!' He shifted so that Flick could see.

'Is he okay? Can we climb in and get him?' Flick was already clambering over the rock. 'I'll try to reach. Shine your torch for me.'

'Watch it, I'm coming too.'

Morris followed Flick into the opening. It was a very wide, deep overhanging rock, and the ground sloped so they were able to stand up as they went further in. Even the shadows seemed to be less as they moved forward.

'Light must be filtering in through gaps in the rock around the edges,' Morris said, glancing around. AT spat and miaowed ungraciously as they approached. 'Here, come on now.'

Morris reached out to touch AT, but the cat bolted between them and shot out into daylight. 'Stupid animal. He was fine all along,' he said with disgust, shining his torch around.

On one side, the rock projected from the overhang's roof, reaching down almost to the floor. Behind it was darkness. He edged forward, feeling Flick's breath on his neck as she tried to see, too. A bigger crevice seemed to slope away into the darkness, into the middle of Hairy Craig itself, as if it were a tunnel heading back to the Law.

Morris suddenly had an idea. All the things he'd been thinking about earlier, before AT turned up, became clear. *Why didn't I think of it before!*

Flick pushed up close to Morris's arm and peered into the gap where the narrow torch beam shone. 'I bet there's buried treasure or something in there. I can get my torch, too,' she yelled excitedly, right in Morris's ear.

'No, that's silly!' said Morris. 'Let's get out of here.'

Treasure was the furthest thing from his mind. He was thinking of dragons. He'd realised just now that this tunnel might lead towards the layr and the trapped dragons. Hadn't Scordril said that only humans – overgrounders – could get through the magic barrier?

He couldn't risk Flick going through it and coming face to face with a dragon. He'd agreed that with Scordril.

But it was different for him. He, Morris, should at least get a look at a dragon before it was all over. After all, he'd helped them by lending the shard, and he might never get another chance. He frowned.

As he led the way out, his mind worked quickly. He was certain now that he wanted to go back in by himself and see if he could find a way through to the dragon layr. But how to get rid of Flick?

And then there was the added problem that if Scordril was around the Law tonight, trying to release the barrier, he couldn't let Flick come back then, either. This was going to be tricky.

As they scrambled back outside and headed to their abandoned picnic site, Morris tried his best to argue against returning at all, but nothing he said worked.

Flick wouldn't be swayed. Folding her arms, she glared obstinately at him. 'I don't care what you say, I want to come back!'

He glared back, aware that his fists were clenched, which seemed slightly ridiculous except that he knew what was at stake. 'Well, I don't. We'd never get permission. It's not safe. We could disturb–'

'Fine! We won't come, we won't have any fun and we won't find any treasure. We can just sit in our tents for the rest of the holiday!' Flick's voice grew shriller. Even the reappearance of AT, no worse for wear, now calmly brushing around her legs, didn't soothe her temper. If anything it spurred her on.

She stood her ground beside the packed picnic stuff.

'See? Even AT prefers me! He's got more nerve than you have. You won't come back when it's dark; you won't come back at all. Well, I think you're a scaredy-cat!'

With that, Flick hoisted her rucksack onto one shoulder, the rug across her other shoulder, and turned and stalked away, back towards the Law. Or rather it would've been stalking if she hadn't kept stumbling under the weight of everything. AT gave a long hard feline stare at Morris, then, tail straight up in the air, followed Flick.

If it weren't so serious, those two would be funny, Morris thought to himself, resisting the urge to laugh, as the two of them walked away. He felt very bad about arguing with Flick, but she rarely stayed in a huff for long. He'd think about her tomorrow. *Besides, I am going back in right now.*

━◦◦◦━

Each step forward took Morris deeper into the tunnel. Further away from the dim light filtering into the cavernous space behind him. Deeper and deeper into the pitch-black darkness that stretched before him. The thin beam from his small torch pierced the gloom and showed that the ground was beginning to slope more steeply. He knew he must tread warily on the uneven surface.

At first, if he stretched his arms out wide, he could place his fingers, or palms, on each side of the tunnel to steady himself. But the tunnel seemed to be widening, and he didn't want to stumble and knock his head. Not now he was on his own.

He had left his rucksack carefully hidden behind a low hump in the first cavern. So, even if Flick came back – and he didn't think she would, in her huff – there would be no sign of him outside and she couldn't follow. She wouldn't expect him to have gone underground, not after their argument.

Automatically, he found himself listening for noises as he pressed on. But all he could hear was the scrape of stone under his boots or the dropping of a fragment of rock as he brushed against it. Everything echoed with a flat, dull sound, around the walls and above him, almost as if a pillow muffled his head. Still, he knew he was listening for a sound that wasn't his boots on stone.

He half-smiled at the realisation that he didn't really know what he was listening for. What exactly did a dragon sound like, he wondered? Scordril – the dragon part of Roderick that had rescued Flick – had come and gone quickly and quietly. No roaring, snarling, or snapping of jaws as the stories said. But even as he thought it, he knew he was being silly. These dragons were trapped, weren't they? And trapped dragons would need food… His mouth felt dry. The skin on the back of his neck prickled as he thought of all the things dragons might do if they had a mind. Well, he'd simply have to hope that they, like Scordril, could understand overgrounder speech – and that he would get a chance to tell them that rescue was on its way. That would stop them eating him, surely?

Nervously, Morris stopped and swung the torch

from side to side. The tunnel seemed to curve sharply up ahead, as if turning directly towards the Law – though he was a little disorientated and might be wrong.

He guessed he must be very deep underground now. The air was cooler. A draught gently tickled his face. He took several steps forward and shivered in the growing chill. He wished he'd put on his proper pullover, not just a sleeveless thing over his summer shirt. *Smart move, dashing down here to get to the dragons without even the proper clothing!* Morris bit his lip and played the torchlight around again.

He gasped. The tunnel seemed to have split into two, no, three separate tunnels. They led away into the blackness. Was the slight draught coming from them? A bit like the wind blowing through the train station in Edinburgh, he thought.

He shook himself, partly to keep warm and partly to dispel the tiniest hint of doubt that was growing inside. Well, here goes, he thought and resolutely continued forward into the middle tunnel.

At the back of his mind he knew that draughts had to come from somewhere, like an open door, or a gateway. Maybe he was getting close to the dragon layr…

But he'd barely taken a dozen paces when the tunnel split again. This time there were many choices. He took one that he felt headed towards the Law. But he was beginning to get more confused now and wasn't really sure. His palms were sweating and in his mind he heard his father's voice, telling him this was a stupid idea – just like he'd told Flick. Morris began to wish that she were here. At least then they could talk to each other. He began to wish he were back at home in Musselburgh. Or in his tent near the dig. Or anywhere but here.

He was so busy thinking that he almost walked into the wall of rocks. A huge heap of stones blocked his way, rising up towards the ceiling of the tunnel, but not quite blocking the tunnel completely. A roof fall?

He half expected a rumbling sound and another fall of stones to bury him any second. Perhaps he could climb through the gap at the top and continue? There was certainly fresher air on the other side because he could feel it.

While he was still wondering what might be on the other side, he heard a noise. He tensed.

There it was again. A slipping, scuffling noise. Falling stones – or something else, something in the tunnel with him. He couldn't be sure how near or far it was.

The hair on his head stood on end. Any remaining confidence evaporated.

Desperately he flashed light around, directing the beam upward to the gaping hole at the top of the rubble. His hands trembled as he imagined a pair of dragon eyes peering down at him. He tried to move but his legs wobbled alarmingly. This was becoming dangerous. He'd wanted to find the layr but he'd never get in this way. He ought to go back before something worse happened.

His legs obeyed him better once he turned away

from the heap of rock. Cold with fear, his teeth chattering, he walked faster and faster, nearly breaking into a run back to the last joining of the tunnels. Fine, now which way! He couldn't remember. He turned one way then another. It all looked the same.

Then he heard the noise again. It was closer. Morris stared helplessly towards the sound. His hands shook so much, he dropped the torch and the light went out. Panic-stricken, he scrabbled on the ground for it. His hands closed on the metal object and he grabbed it, clutched it to his chest, and struggled to switch it on again.

Two golden-green eyes stared at him in the darkness. He thrust the torch out like a weapon in front of him, but immediately he was knocked flying. Moist, warm breath hit his face and he grabbed a tuft of fur. Something sharp dug into his flesh as he struggled. Then there was a loud yowl right in his ear.

He shone the torch at the sound – and AT's furry face snarled back. Tears of relief sprang to Morris's eyes. 'AT!' Morris yelled in relief, trying to hug the large cat. AT hissed and wrestled himself clear.

Once Morris had calmed down, he gazed at the cat. If AT had come in, it couldn't be too difficult to get out. His confidence restored by the company, Morris looked about, ready to pick a tunnel. 'Law behind, sea where? It's not you, or you…' He pointed at his final choice, muttering, 'That has to be the one heading back towards Hairy Craig.' He stepped forward and almost fell as AT blocked his path. 'Move, clear out…' He said, trying to push past the cat. AT simply pushed harder against Morris's legs. After a few moments of pushing at each other, AT sped away up one of the tunnels. Then he darted back to Morris as quickly as he'd left.

'Mmm… I wonder…' Morris murmured, stepping towards the tunnel AT had chosen. This time there was no pushing and AT settled to walk alongside Morris. 'You know the way, don't you?' Morris glanced at the cat, but AT just flicked his tail and ran ahead. Convinced that the cat did know the way out, Morris followed, puffing slightly as the ground started to rise. Soon they were at the place where the tunnel split into three.

'Which way now, AT?' Morris asked. But AT did nothing.

Annoyed, Morris made to go up the left-hand tunnel. AT reacted with a hiss and ran across Morris's feet, his tail flipping across the scratches he'd made on the boy's shin earlier.

Morris waited as AT turned and ambled confidently up the middle tunnel. 'So, that's the one. Why didn't you say?'

With AT guiding him, he was soon back at the shallow cave and collecting his bag. Morris had never been as happy to sniff fresh air, and see the sky and countryside. 'Good teamwork!' he said, smiling down at AT. But he knew that without AT he might never have got out of the tunnels. AT was the real hero. What if the batteries in the torch had failed? Morris shivered at the thought. He'd been lucky.

He ran around like a maniac, waving his arms like

windmill sails. AT took one look and disappeared down the side of the Craig.

Morris knew he had to get back to the camp; it was starting to grow dusky. He knew he'd been wrong to go off without telling, especially when he was going underground, and he'd be missed if he didn't return. *Besides*, he thought, *I've missed supper.*

Flick poked her head through the flap of her tent almost as soon as she heard Morris untying his. 'You're for it!' she hissed across at him. 'Your mum was here looking for you. Where on earth did you get to?'

Morris grimaced at the thought of punishment chores. 'Just round and about... lost track of time. I found AT again, though,' he said, changing the subject.

Flick made a low 'humph' and retreated into her tent. Her muffled voice reached him through the canvas. 'By the way, there's a scone under your pyjamas.'

Morris smiled and clambered into the safety of his little tent.

———•••———

Scordril was exceedingly tired after the day's preparations of the special magic – too tired, in fact, for the release plan to be put into action tonight. And now he'd had to morph, too. All he could think about, as he caught his breath in the camping field, was how he hated having to morph into Roderick, having to walk not fly, especially when he was in such a rush.

He sank quietly down to his knees on the dry grass,

staring at the closed tent flaps. There was no sound from inside. He sensed that the boy was already asleep.

Not wanting to scare Morris by pushing his head inside the tent without warning, yet not wishing to disturb the girl, Flick, by calling out, instinctively the dragon inside Roderick sought for Morris with his mind. *»Morris, Morris... Wake up...»* He heard the sound of Morris yawning and moving about inside.

Roderick took his chance, and pushed his face towards the opening in the tent.

'Morris, it's Roderick... May I enter? I came to return your shard,' he whispered, as loud as he dared. Then, without waiting for the answer he pushed his way into the tent.

Morris, rubbing his eyes, sat cross-legged on his makeshift bed. He looked pale and tired, but not surprised. 'Hello, come in. Funny, I was just thinking about you,' he mumbled, moving his rucksack to make more room.

Smiling, Roderick sat down where Morris pointed, wondering what he should say first. Everything he had to say was important. 'You are tired?' he began.

'Must've dozed off. Busy day, you know.' Morris ran his fingers through his untidy hair, shaking himself. 'Didn't expect to see you today. It worked, then, the magic?'

Roderick nodded and fished around in his shirt pocket, below his sweater. Keeping his voice low and listening for any noises from the other tent or any approaching overgrounders, Roderick produced the pottery shard. 'Here... Thank you. I – we – are extremely grateful,' he said, handing the pottery over to Morris like a trophy. 'It worked better than I had imagined. But, please, accept my apologies for the colour,' Roderick added, watching Morris closely, to see how the boy reacted to the changes.

'Thanks.' Morris turned the shard over and over. 'It looks, um, different.' He stared at Roderick. 'Smaller?'

'Yes. I had to remove a fragment to use in the first spell. Then the rest changed colour in the main spell.'

'I helped with magic!' Morris said, his voice low like Roderick's. But his eyes looked more alert now and he met Roderick's gaze proudly. 'And, you came today, after all! I was worried I'd miss you if you came tomorrow. Flick and I, we're going into Edinburgh with my parents, you see. Won't be back until late.'

'Oh…' Roderick felt his strangely smooth skin prickle when he thought what might have happened if he'd missed Morris.

'Can you tell me about the spell? Did it save the dragons?' Morris sounded eager to hear about the magic.

Resting his hands on his knees, Roderick took a deep breath. 'That is the other thing I came to say, Morris. We haven't removed the barrier yet. We have to recover our full strength to use the magic we've made. It's very powerful and dangerous. I came to warn you to stay in your tent tomorrow night… Flick, too,' he added quickly.

'No problem. We'll be shattered after our trip, I guess.' Morris frowned. 'Is that when you're going to do it?'

'Yes,' said Roderick, his voice stern now. He

reached out and gripped Morris's shoulder. 'You must both stay out of the way. Tomorrow night, many of the dragons of Musselburgh will be at Traprain Law with me, Morris. And we will be dragons, not overgrounders. We must be dragons to use the spell. Tomorrow night we will rescue our kin in Traprain.'

CHAPTER 8

Dragongrid

The sun had long set by the time the wing of dragons under Kvayn's command flew east from Musselburgh one glow later. Scordril had fretted until his eyes whirred glitters of silver and white and Threah had to admonish him for wasting the reserves he was building up.

»*They will not starve today if they survived yesterday,*« she said severely. »*I shall send young Zefion to you if this continues. You are putting us all at risk, never mind the Traprain Law dragonkin.*«

»*I do not need to be calmed by a dragon who broadcasts soothing pictures of meadows and cavern fires,*« Scordril roared, forgetting momentarily how much Threah disliked his outbursts of temper. »*I merely wish to get on with it and be done... It is a pity we cannot use magepower to bring night on early. Besides,*« he said, sniffing the air noisily, »*even down here I can tell that the air is changing, and that rain will start to come in from over the sea. It bodes ill for our task.*«

He'd been right. Large splashes of rain fell intermittently as they flew in formation high above

Tranent and the surrounding meadows and on past Haddington. Their dragonsight allowed them to see where they were heading but they took no precautions to conceal their flight. The storm clouds that were gathering like huge dirty piles of sheepskins were enough to camouflage them from any overgrounder who happened to be out on such a night – which was not likely, reflected Scordril, turning his head slightly to check that the others were still with him.

Androtta, the recorder, and Vanurl, his older assistant, had decided to remain in the Musselburgh layr. The wing consisted, therefore, of the mages Kvayn, Fenror, Ygdrann and himself flying in pairs as outriders; Threah, who had with her a skin of healing herbals; young Ennasif, who was to help Threah when and if necessary and who, if Scordril was reading it right, was beginning to show elementary magepower; Zefion with his projecting powers; and Minikk, who would carry a message back to the layr after they had freed the Traprain Law dragons.

Minikk and Ennasif were inseparable at the moment, sighed Scordril to himself, thinking about the two young females – though they were starting to take more interest in the younger male dragons in the layr, as indeed these males were of them! He glanced over at Threah and felt his heart warm, despite the squalls and showers.

At the centre of the wing flew Brygnon and Emblir – the latter being the strongest female in the layr – who carried between them, like an overgrounder hammock, a net of stout fibres torn from animal hides. In it, Fenror had placed the large rock he had found the glow before, now filled with a magic that exactly matched the strange one that had resulted from mixing ancient magics with Brekk's own embryonic mage power.

Directly behind Brygnon and Emblir flew Gylning of Traprain Law, his wing looking much better now. He was clearly staying sufficiently close to them to make certain the rock would arrive at its destination and his kin be rescued! He was showing a fine turn of humour now that he was so much improved, and his bruises and gashes were healing. It was he who'd asked if they ought to take with them, and replant, the uprooted clump of dragongrid that Scordril had used to try out the magic. *»There's a hole in the turf that may cause us to trip one day,»* he pointed out, tongue in cheek.

They landed on the west side of the Law in a draught of wingbeats that rivalled the gale that was blowing up. Fenror, squat and muscular, immediately spoke. *»I saw no sign of movement or light from anyone in the camp of the overgrounder boy,»* he said. *»But with this wind, our task is made more difficult. We should get started quickly.»* His darting, watchful eyes continued to survey the terrain and skies around them even as he spoke. *»I keep thinking those black clouds are magic covers for nightdragons and wingriders. It makes my hide crawl.»*

As if to refute his point, thunder rumbled in the distance but there had been no lightning as yet and Kvayn said, *»In that case, we must get on and release the dragongrid so that our kin will be able help us fight them off.»*

Scordil pointed. *»The barrier is two wing-spans in*

that direction» He sounded calmer than he felt. Was Zefion already projecting? »*When we are all closer, the mages must be in front and the others remain behind us for safety.*»

Threah came up to him as they tramped slowly across the field. Her blue-grey scales glistened in the damp. »*Will the rain affect the safety of the magic-casting?*» she queried, clearly concerned for him as well as for the outcome.

»*I cannot truthfully say,*» Scordril answered her on a tight mindlink. »*But I must go ahead. It is the only solution we have thought of. And at least it has been tried.*»

The mages signalled to the others to stop where they were and moved forward by themselves. Kvayn's grey face looked unusually drawn, but otherwise Scordril could sense they were in good heart. He, too, felt better now that the time had come.

»*Stay here,*» he ordered, and went to push at the barrier with his snout. He felt the resistance and the strange taste in his mouth but suddenly, too, relief from worry. They had the means of sorting this out once and for all. They would not stand for such evil.

———⟨∅∅∅⟩———

The dragongrid operation was barely underway when the storm began raging round them in earnest. Fenror, Kvayn and Ygdrann were soon standing in mud, and the rock positioned by Emblir and Brygnon became isolated by a small channel of water that rippled in two forks around it before joining again to flow away past Scordril.

Scordril himself was tightly shielded, wrapped in a web of fine tendrils of magic, several layers deep, and focused on redirecting the store of strange magic sent to him by the other mages. At the edge of his awareness he sensed their concentration, but his mind had to deflect the alien magic in such a way that the inverted stream hit first the nearby section of grid and then moved on north, north-east, east, as he mentally traced the barrier's position. This took all his concentration.

Only a quarter of a glow-mark would be needed to complete the banishment of the grid. As the successive implosions flared round the part they could see from where they were, Scordril thought it looked remarkably like the fuse of one of the overgrounder firetoys they lit in Musselburgh at the start of winter each sun-round.

He closed his eyes as the line of sight disappeared. He had to trace it now by sensing instead. This was much more tiring because most of his energy was already linked into maintaining his protective mesh. As the circle of bright white flares came round the south side of the Law and into sight again, he felt himself weaken, knew he was drawing on his last reserves of magepower, and held onto his task with gritted teeth and clamped jaw. He hadn't time to consider the others. So long as they supplied him with alien magic from the stone, he would continue.

Then – like a dragon swooping to kill – tongues of

forked lightning flashed from the sky above Traprain Law, illuminating the countryside for miles around, blinding them with yellow, orange, white streaks. He felt the web around him move, just a slight tug, a barely perceptible shift in his armour – but it opened his shielding to the magic and he knew he was done for.

In the same instant, he felt the presence of Gylning in his mind. Gylning? What the—? And the web closed, his shielding was restored and the last implosion rivalled the faded lightning as the dragongrid collapsed completely and Traprain Law was freed.

Scordril sank down where he was, heedless of the mud on his bronze scales, now turned to dull brown. His snout fell forward and everything went black.

Moments later, when he returned woozily to the dark, wet night and the sound of rain on his hide, he was surrounded by four weary dragons – one of whom looked like Gylning.

»*Gylning?*« he groaned through his headpain, forcing his heavy lids to open wide enough to see Gylning's pale green eyes properly. »*You could have told us before.*«

»*I didn't know, myself,*« confessed the young dragon, looking somewhat astonished still, »*until I saw you flinch. I was concentrating on you, yes, but I did not know I could help... Are you all right?*«

»*All right? I have discovered a mage! Why would I not be all right? Come here, youngone. You saved my life.*«

Threah pushed through the group, carrying a skin vessel of steaming feverfew tincture. Thrusting it at

Scordril's snout, she lifted his top jaw and simply poured it down his throat. »*Quickest way to get you well,*» she said tersely. »*We can't carry you in – even if we knew where to go.*»

Gylning spoke up. »*I'll show you the shortest route... when Scordil has regained his strength, that is,*» he said helpfully, as if he wanted the topic of his suddenly emerged mage power forgotten. Scordril thought Gylning was somewhat in awe of him and grimaced. He would take the youngone under his wing and bring him on fast – they would need all the magepower they had shortly, if their guesses were correct about the wingriders' intentions.

Fenror said, »*I knew it would kill you, Scordril. No one could foresee the storm. I for one am glad for Gylning's intervention. We could not ourselves know of the need.*»

»*Don't worry about me, Fenror,*» said Scordril, struggling to his feet and inspecting each limb in turn, stretching and twisting them to test the muscles, then flexing his wings gently. »*I am intent on getting into Traprain layr and finding out what they used those ancient pots for. Without Morris's shard, this rescue would not have been accomplished. And I have a feeling we might need his help yet again. Though that may be just a silly whim while my head is not quite sound.*»

The dragon wing reassembled round Gylning as the first tiny sign of light grew over the eastern horizon. Aware of the urgency due to the short nights, they quickly followed him to the nearest entrance, which was cleverly hidden in the middle of a grove of prickly bushes, exactly the sort of thing that overgrounders would fear to push through. They pushed in without a problem, and Scordril let his breath out audibly – he realised he had still doubted their success.

They walked only a half dragonspan into the tunnel before a roar greeted them from within, echoing round their ears and filling them with pride and excitement. Two dragons appeared out of the darkness.

»*Njortin,*» cried Gylning, rushing forward. »*And Thofirin! We have come. The dragongrid is smashed...*» He stopped and turned round, gesturing with one claw to his companions. »*This is Dragonmaster Kvayn and the dragons of Musselburgh layr. We have so much to tell you.*»

———∽∾∿∾———

»*Welcome, Dragonmaster Kvayn, and dragonkin of Musselburgh! Welcome, and a million sun-rounds of thanks from grateful Traprain!*»

Njortin's dark eyes twinkled with joy as he looked from dragon to dragon, his mindspeech loud enough to be heard above the roar from the tunnel behind. Then, stepping forward to face Kvayn, he bowed low until his long snout touched the ground.

Thofirin followed his lead and then, seemingly, had to help him straighten up by grasping his left forearm. Gylning rushed forward, but wasn't as quick as Kvayn who stretched out her arm and took Njortin's other side.

»*Greetings, Njortin. We are glad to answer your brave*

messenger Gylning's call.» She turned to Gylning and he seemed to grow visibly taller, or so Scordril thought, watching, as Kvayn continued. »*And I, I am glad to return,*» she said, before acting in an undragonmasterly fashion and rubbing snouts lovingly with Njortin and then Thofirin. The rescued dragons, who had held back in the tunnel behind Njortin, began to push forward.

Scordril, still shaky after his narrow escape from the lightning, and suddenly fearing he would be swamped and suffocated by his Traprain Law kin, stepped back, looking nervously over his shoulder to the way back overground.

But Fenror, Brygnon and Emblir quickly pushed in front of Kvayn and Gylning, and began to greet the other Traprain dragons. A great confusion of dragons began, with much pushing and shoving.

Oblivious to what was going on around them, Kvayn, Njortin and Thofirin, their heads close, continued to confer, but privately now with a tight mindlink that Scordril could not hear. A few Traprain dragons were allowed through. They nodded as they passed him, and rushed out towards the fresh air overground. Scordril only sensed one name he recognised, Sygnadi, as the dragons dashed by. Scordril thought there would be many things needed from outside, food, firewood…

Ygdrann bent towards Gylning and seemed to whisper something to the young dragon, who nodded vigorously, and then they headed the other way, into the layr.

Scordril wondered why, then saw that they were organising the Traprain dragons into two lines at the widest part of the inner tunnel, just ahead, ready to greet the rescuers as honoured dragonguests.

So, proudly, and to more roars and cheers, the Musselburgh dragons were shown into the Traprain layr. Kvayn walked between Njortin and Thofirin. Gylning joined in part way and walked beside Thofirin.

Scordril forgot all about the dangers that he had just faced and began to enjoy the experience, although the noise in the layr was so loud it gave him headpain. He turned back and saw the other Musselburgh dragons falling into line behind him.

As he walked, he glanced at the faces of the rescued dragons. They were happy, yes, but he saw and sensed the fear that had gripped them. Some of the older faces were tired and thin.

As he walked on towards the centre of the layr he found himself guessing at the ordeal that the Traprain Council had had to oversee. He knew what he would have done in their place – ration air-dried meat usually stored in the furthest, coolest chamber for winter, and share it out amongst the oldest and the youngest dragons. Post watchdragons to warn of a change in the barrier's magic. Or an intruder! Tell everyone else to rest and conserve their energy, gathering them together for warmth and to save firewood. Desperately trying to concentrate on the hope of rescue…

The tunnel suddenly widened. There were more tunnels off in all directions and the parade of dragons swept forward. Someone up ahead had fetched more torches and he saw Gylning take one, then breathe on it to light it.

Then there, before Scordril, was the entrance to the Great Chamber. An ornate wooden door covered in jewels and metal stood open. His dragonsight was dazzled by copper and silver swirls shaped into dragons, with stones – dragonblood-red – as eyes. This was the place he had read of in the Chronicles. The door even smelled of ancient dragon magic. Scordril almost ran forward, his eyes whirring, to see what it was like inside, just stopping himself at the last. *You are older than an eager youngone! And a mage!* he told himself, but his excitement was real.

The leading dragons had entered the chamber, down several wide steps. He could see over their heads. He let his breath out in astonishment, as a flickering stream of tiny golden flames…

A curving hall, carved from the rock by dragonbreath, spread out before him, like a bigger version of the Great Hall at home, but otherwise as unlike Musselburgh as a fish is to an eagle. Scordril had never seen anything like it. The walls and floor were coloured! Even in the poor, flickering light from three golden torches hung on the wall opposite the door, he could see that much.

The floor was more vibrant than the colour of the soil in the fields between Musselburgh and the Law. It was a warm red-brown, worn with years of treading claws, and trailing tails, deepening to a rich orange-red around the fire-pit sunk in the middle of the floor. Scordril slowed to a standstill at the foot of the steps, barely noticing that other Musselburgh dragons did the same. The colour ran up the walls and changed in shade, paler in places, then richer like a mix of autumn leaves, blending into the contours of the melted rocks. But the section of wall with the torches was darkest, vivid, blood red and sparkling with specks of gold, a shimmering metallic dust of real gold.

Threah, almost walking into him, met his eyes as she looked around, her jaw hanging open. Scordril saw the wonder he was feeling reflected in Threah's face. »*It's so, so beautiful...*» Her mindspeech was hushed. He barely heard it amongst the din around them.

Dragons hurrying in from behind with scrubby firewood began building up the shallow, weak fire in the pit. Scordril saw Zefion rush past to help.

It took no time at all before the space started warming through and dragons were being sent here and there. Threah had taken herself off to one side of the chamber and was seeing who, if anyone, needed help. A small queue of anxious dragons was forming. Ennasif was near her, along with Minikk. A male Traprain dragon was watching them intently.

Alone for a moment, gazing around, Scordril felt his chest swell with pride. Not only had the rescue been successful but dragonkin from each layr were working together to speedily return Traprain to normal. Thinking of dragonkin, he remembered that the news still had to be passed back home.

»*I believe it is time for you to go, Minikk,*» Scordril announced.

Minikk was watching Ennasif as she applied a soothing herbal balm to a sickly looking youngone. Minikk was assigned to go back to Musselburgh and tell the dragons there that the rescue had worked, but she wasn't moving. In fact, she should already have asked to go back, not waited to be told.

Scordril felt his temper bubbling up inside and wrinkled his snout with disgust. *»Our layr is waiting for news of our success, Minikk,»* Scordril snapped. He was sure that Minikk glanced swiftly at Ennasif first and rolled her eyes, before nodding and beginning to move. Youngones!

Threah seemed to have guessed his annoyance as she swiftly caught Minikk and laid her claws on the young dragon's shoulders.

»Once the news is delivered, Minikk, be sure to tell Androtta exactly what happened. He will record your own account. You will be named in the Chronicles.» Threah returned Scordril's gaze with a smile. *»Ennasif will stay here with me...»*

»I will go as fast as my wings can carry me, Threah... Scordil...» Minikk nodded to each as she addressed them, then quickening her step, headed to the doorway.

One more task sorted. Scordril wondered now where the other mages had got to, then, recognising Njortin in his mind, turned to see the wise, long-snouted face behind him, about to address the chamber. It had been a long night for both of them.

»To you a special thanks, Scordril. Kvayn has told me of your bravery. And Gylning of your trust.»

Scordril sensed the strength of the old mage's gratitude as Njortin's dark blue-grey face smiled, showing his yellowed, worn teeth. He also sensed that Njortin knew everything that had happened in the rescue – from Gylning saving his life, to having shown some emerging magepower.

»As for the mages of Traprain,» Njortin announced to the assembled dragons, *»we wish to invite all those who would come, as our kin, to celebrate our freedom and reward our rescuers.»*

Kvayn nodded at once, and Scordril found himself agreeing just as quickly. Njortin formally introduced his dragonmate, Thofirin, to all the newcomers; but as he did so, Scordril grew restless knowing there were serious matters to discuss. Even the astute Njortin didn't know of the fears the Musselburgh council had about the nightdragons and wingriders. It would be foolish to celebrate when we should prepare for an attack, Scordil thought.

Once Njortin had finished, and as if reading Scordril's mind, Kvayn gestured with her wing to the ledge around the wall, below the torches. *»Come, Scordril, and you, too, Njortin. Let us sit over here. I sense there are many things Scordril wishes to say.»*

Scordril noted that Kvayn's grey face looked more powerful than ever as he followed her past the fire. Still, perhaps it was coming back to her birth-layr that made her seem that way. He sat on her left, facing the door, with Njortin and Thofirin on her right. For once, Scordril was pleased that Zefion had filled the area before them with a real fire, and not merely his calming images. They were joined by two others, Gullfi and Skolfari – twin brothers, and mages, Njortin explained. So alike that it was only the exceptionally pale grass-green eyes of Gullfi that separated him from his darker-eyed brother. Their greeting, spoken almost as one dragon, was so loud it left Scordril's mind ringing and added to his headpain. But they were quickly sent away by Njortin to see to other tasks. Scordril watched as the twins joined Ygdrann and Fenror, talking together near the door, then were led away to a shadowy tunnel entrance at the far side of the chamber.

»*Now is not the time for a council meeting, Scordril,*» Njortin began, turning his head back to Scordril. »*But I want to know how you removed the barrier. Gylning has sent me many strange images, and spoken briefly of your concern that its removal will attract the invaders. Yet he hinted in his mind about other more dreadful concerns you have. He has gone with Brygnon, I understand, to replace a piece of turf.*» He shook his head. »*No matter, I wish to discuss these things with you.*»

Scordril found himself explaining everything to Njortin and Thofirin, whilst Kvayn sat claws on knees. He briefly described the arrival of Gylning and the discussions at the Musselburgh council. Njortin listened with his head on one side, nodding, as Scordril spoke.

»*After Gylning explained about the magic blocking his way, and the Musselburgh council decided we needed to learn more before we could act, I spent a long night reading the Traprain Chronicles written by Fargelmir.*»

Seemingly pleased to hear that the Chronicles were safe, Njortin interrupted.

»*You must tell this to our current recorder, Kyrekk, later today.*»

Scordril noticed an odd look pass over Kvayn's face as Njortin spoke, and Njortin added, »*Kyrekk is half-sister to Kvayn. She remained here after the Great Split.*«

Scordril found it difficult to tell a straight story after that – he was often interrupted by either Thofirin or Njortin, as they asked question after question. They were concerned about the suggestion that the barrier magic had matured and that the nightdragons, driven by their wingriders, might return. They also wanted to know about Gylning's idea, that replacing the spell with something of their own making might fool the nightdragons, who seemed to have no magics. This might give Traprain Law time to prepare for war.

»*We remember the invaders,*« Thofirin said, scraping her claws together and looking around at the others. »*It was a bitter time for the layr. We hoped they would not return... So many dragon lives lost. And for what? To fight again?*«

Njortin shook his head and frowned before looking directly into Scordril's eyes. »*But you are correct in your reasoning, Scordril. I have sensed the evil woven into the spell.*« Njortin pressed his thin lips together. »*We need to outwit our enemy... Go on, please. How did you defeat the barrier? It may give us an idea of the next step.*«

Scordril tried to outline the weaving of the spell. Njortin was especially interested to hear that a pottery fragment had been involved, and not at all amazed that an overgrounder had helped. »*That, from what I see in your mind, is part of a bowl brought here many centuries ago, by a grateful 'before', one of the early overgrounders, for our ancients to use.*«

»*My other concern,*» Scordril went on quietly, »*is that other overgrounders may find pottery fragments left behind, lost by the ancients. There is a group out there now digging with just such an intent – though they know nothing of dragons. What if they find one and discover its power in years to come?*»

The silence that hung in the air as he paused told him how dreadful such a prospect was to the others.

Nevertheless, the immediate threat had to be dealt with first. Scordril lost track of how long he talked, but by the end of it they all agreed that their own magic should be used to erect another look-alike grid as a matter of urgency. This would fool any nightscout probing it from a distance into thinking their own enclosing grid was unbroken. They agreed to do this as soon as they had rested and regained full mage strength.

They discussed the best way to make the new grid.

Thofirin suddenly clapped. »*I have it! We can weave a special door-lock spell, one which we can open and close, but no other can!*»

Murmurs of approval followed.

»*We can use a dragon image from our door, instead of your clump of grass,*» she added, turning to face Scordril. »*That is also ancient magework and will seem to them the same, if they sense it from afar.*»

Scordril decided Thofirin's idea would work so he agreed to help her with it.

Talk then turned to the celebration that Njortin had mentioned. Scordril scratched his snout and said, »*If we are to be busy weaving a spell today, then two days from now is the earliest we can have the celebration if we are to prepare properly.*»

That, too, was agreed and the group rose to go and talk to their own kin, and, in Scordril's case, to rest. The others would rest as soon as their chores were finished but Scordril's mage powers were depleted and he would be working with Thofirin soon.

As Kvayn rose, she seemed to freeze, staring at something, her wings half open. Scordril tried to see what she was looking at. A dragon had entered the chamber, and carried a bowl of water over to Threah and Ennasif, still working at the far side. The dragon handed over the bowl and then turned, heading for a tunnel at the very end of the hall.

»*Jarl?*» hissed Kvayn.

Scordril looked at Njortin and Thofirin. Their heads dipped, then they both moved away, Thofirin drawing Kvayn to her side with a gesture. Scordril was left on his own for a moment, suddenly thinking again about Jarl and the Chronicles and what may or may not have been the truth all those years ago.

Then he walked over to Ennasif and a Traprain male who was talking as he helped her.

Ennasif was saying, »*Before that is all gone, Yorheim, will you show me the water spring? Then we will bring back as much as we can carry.*»

»*Certainly. The spring is deep under the layr, in an outer cavern. We were thankful we had it when we were imprisoned,*» Yorheim said.

Threah looked at Scordril, her eyes holding a mischievous glint that puzzled Scordril until he sensed the mixture of emotions, shyness, gratitude and something else – affection? – emanating from Ennasif.

»*Ah, so! It will be an interesting time here at Traprain,*« he sent to Threah on a tight link. »*But right now, I need to rest and then help with the replacement grid and then replenish my powers before visiting the overgrounder camp. There's something I need to ask Morris. I'll be back at the layr tonight. Make sure Ennasif flies too!*«

————

Morris looked up from the billycan of bubbling soup and stopped stirring. Something was wrong. Something to do with the bush that was in his line of vision and probably the length of a football pitch away from him – a very wet one at that, with puddles still drying out.

He peered again across the field, shielding his eyes against the setting sun. It was still weak and lacking in warmth after the previous night's storm, but bright enough to make him squint awkwardly.

There! It happened again. Something had moved near the bush – the trouble was, everything had the sun behind it so the bush was merely a deep black silhouette.

He rubbed his eyes and slopped the soup around the pan twice more, then took it off the flames, and set the billycan on the grass to cool. He hated burning his tongue on scalding soup.

In an effort to not look across the field for one whole minute, he sat the kettle on the flames instead and heaped two spoons of cocoa in through the spout. He and Flick had taken to boiling up cocoa for a nighttime drink. She'd be back before it was ready, since the flames were dying down now and giving off less heat.

When he finally dared look again across the field, he nearly jumped out of his skin. The bush was definitely nearer than it had been. He could make out the branches, which he hadn't been able to before. Come to think of it, he wasn't sure he could remember there having been a bush over there.

But that was impossible. He stared again, screwing up his eyes so much he gave himself a headache. Even as his heart started to thump uncomfortably and his hand grew clammy, a flash of something waved briefly at the side of the bush before disappearing.

He was imagining it. They'd spent too long in Craigmillar Castle the day before, investigating the plot to murder Lord Darnley. In fact they'd been discussing plots and weird happenings all today, too, while helping his parents with some final digging. Now he was seeing bushes coming to get him. He suddenly wished he had Flick here with him. But she'd gone off to the village to help her dad with something in the shop.

Then his blood ran cold. The bush was moving towards him. Almost imperceptibly it was coming towards his tent. He jumped to his feet and backed away from the fire, too frightened to scream.

Catching his foot on the guy rope behind him, he sat heavily on the grass.

»*Morris!*»

This was it, then. He'd gone loony. He was hearing voices in his head. He shut his eyes tight and held his breath, waiting for the bush to attack.

»*Morris! It's Roderick. Where is your friend?*»

Morris let his breath out all in a rush, faint with relief. Scordril and a magic bush! He'd murder the man!

'It's okay,' he called shakily. 'She's not here.'

The bush disappeared and there stood Scordril in his usual overgrounder disguise of Roderick.

'Sorry to frighten you. I needed to know if you were alone.'

The sound of Scordril's rough human voice reminded Morris of something. 'You s-spoke in my head! How did you do that? And how did you think I'd answer you if Flick had been here?'

'You would have thought of some way, being a resourceful youngone,' said Scordril gravely. 'And yes, I did speak into your mind. I didn't know if it would work, though I managed to wake you up the last time I tried, if I remember rightly. I need to ask you something—'

'Did you do it?' interrupted Morris, forgetting his fright as he suddenly realised something tremendous had happened the night before while he was sleeping off his tiredness from the day's trip. How could he have forgotten something so important? 'Did you set the dragons free? Was there a big battle?' he asked excitedly.

Scordril fixed him with eyes that seemed to shine gold-green in the fading light. 'There was no battle but there may still be one. That's the bit I haven't told you... Let's sit over here so we can see where everyone is. Please eat your food, though.'

Morris told Scordril about Flick in between quickly slurping the soup from the billycan, in a way his mother would have called disgusting – but he didn't think a dragon would mind. As he filled the pan with water to soak, he said, 'What is it you want to ask? We need to be quick. She'll be here soon.'

'That pottery shard. I don't mind you having it because, as a friend of the dragons, I can trust you to keep it in your possession. What worries me is something else.'

Morris looked at him but said nothing. He was pleased to be called a friend of the dragons but he knew something more was coming, something important.

'There are others in the world who are not as... let's say... scrupulous. Those who would use old dragon artefacts to harm others, overgrounders who do not value old things as treasures to preserve, but who use them to take control of other people. It is most important that we do not let any dragon workings leave this place with your parents when they go.'

'You think there are other pieces like mine?' Morris hadn't thought of that.

'It is quite possible. I want you to help. Besides, it would be safer for everyone if the diggers were not here at all. But I suppose you cannot make that happen.'

'Oh, that's okay, sir...er, Roderick. They're packing up tomorrow and leaving the day after. They've finished. Why, is something going to happen?'

'That's what I haven't told you.'

There was a pause. Morris noticed that Scordril glanced round him, probably checking if anyone was coming their way. But maybe, too, he was wondering how much he could tell a boy. Morris was young but he had never been the sort of boy who gave away secrets.

'You can trust me,' he said.

'I know,' said Scordril, turning back to face him. 'I have never doubted you.'

The sun was on its way to the horizon in a half-hearted display of pink and orange, and a chill breeze started to waft through the field. Morris shivered but Scordril seemed not to be affected. Finally, he appeared to come to a decision.

'Morris, the dragons who were involved in erecting the grid round Traprain Law were renegades from the north who are under the control of the people who ride them. We call them wingriders. We fear they will come back, hoping to take the Lothian dragons prisoner. They will not be able to do so now – thanks to your help. But they may still come, and we are preparing for the worst. That is why I would like there to be no digging here. It is no longer safe for overgrounders.'

'I understand,' said Morris, sobered by the thought of a dragon battle over the Law and bodies falling out of the sky. It seemed like a story. But what had Scordril been saying about other shards?

'You wanted me to help?' he asked, looking confidently at Roderick's overgrounder face as if it were his own father's.

Scordril suddenly flicked his head in a most un-human way as if sniffing the air and piercing it with a long-distance lens. 'Is that your friend Flick?'

Morris could only see a dot far away across the field to the east. It was so dim by now that he could only marvel at Scordril's eyesight.

'Dunno,' he said truthfully. 'But it's possible. I'm expecting her soon. Tell me quickly what you want.'

Scordril lost no time in explaining how he needed Morris to check the archaeological finds that were being taken away.

'You mean, while they're packing them up tomorrow?'

'Any time. Can you get into the store where they are kept? You could do that tomorrow night and then no one would see you and you could look carefully.'

'I would look carefully, anyway,' said Morris indignantly. 'But what am I to look for? The dragon etching?'

'Yes, but I have something to help you. Do you remember I said I would give you a present for helping? Or did I merely think it?'

Scordril was talking fast now and fumbling in his pocket. The dot on the horizon had turned into a human and without doubt it was Flick walking in her usual zigzag fashion back to the tent.

'Here,' said Scordril, handing him something and standing up to go.

Morris looked down at the stone in his hand. It was brown with white veins and quite slim, as if someone had flattened it. The edges were smooth and the whole thing felt heavier than it ought to. He looked questioningly at Scordril. At the same time, he noticed a white mist rolling in around the campsite. How strange that it should come so suddenly.

'This is a talisman,' said Scordril. 'It will call me when you hold it and think urgently of me. Do not speak my name, just call me in your mind and I will come. But if you hold it while you search the artefacts the overgrounders have found, it will vibrate in the presence of dragon magic... I must go. Goodbye, Morris.'

And he disappeared into the mist.

Moments later, as Flick arrived breathlessly, the mist suddenly rolled away and the camp became merely dark and lonely.

'How strange,' murmured Morris, slipping his hand quickly into his pocket.

'What?' asked Flick, untying her tent door and grabbing her nightclothes.

'Nothing... Well, I just wondered about the mist disappearing so suddenly as if it had changed its mind.' In fact, he was wondering if Scordril had had a part in it.

'Oh, mist is like that here,' said Flick, nonchalantly. 'Near the Forth estuary and all that. They come and go like yo-yos. Shall we have our hot chocolate when we've got into bed? We can always wash up in the morning. It's getting horribly cold.'

⸺◦∕◦∕◦⸺

It was horribly cold the next night, too. Not a bit like midsummer, Morris thought, as he crept doggedly across the dew-sodden grass at nearly midnight. A light mist was shielding most of the light from the moon, which was just past its highest point. A tiny amount was shaved off at its ten o'clock position and Morris reckoned it would be full the next night. If there were no clouds to hide it, he might even want to take a look – though if it was as cold as this, he might prefer to stay in his sleeping bag.

He'd pulled on thick socks and tucked the bottoms of his pyjama legs into them to try to keep them dry, and the draught out. And then added a jumper and jacket. But nothing could make his nose feel other than a block of ice.

One hand was in his jacket pocket clutching the strange stone Scordril had given him. He'd not let it out of his sight all day. Which was funny, really, because he only half believed it had any magical powers – at least, when he was with Flick. When he was with Scordril, he could believe anything. After all, with his own eyes he'd seen him as a dragon... Funny, but that seemed weeks ago now, not a matter of a few days.

The two children had spent most of the day helping to clear the site, Morris checking every inch of the ground for tools or other valuable items that might have dropped unnoticed into the grass, and Flick – complaining under her breath – assisting with the packing of canteen equipment into boxes and bags. Only the sleeping tents, the 'finds' tent and the toilet compartment had been left to be dismantled tomorrow.

They'd managed a couple of hours off site, which they'd used to walk once right round the Law as if on patrol, a sort of ending ceremony. Every time they had turned a corner – well, more of a bend, really – Flick had said again that she wished the holiday could go on forever.

This had given Morris the germ of an idea, but he'd not said anything to Flick at the time because his mind was preoccupied with his coming task, wondering how he could slip out to examine the packing cases.

He knew he'd disturbed Flick next door as he'd untied his own little tent.

'Whereyeroff?' she'd called drowsily. 'Amcomingtoo... Wait.'

'The loo... I'm desperate!' Morris had hissed back. 'Stay warm, won't be a moment.'

With relief, he'd heard her turn over and fall silent. Then he'd crept away, circling the site well away from the adults' sleeping tents, torch held straight downwards, leaving only the small patch of grass lit up immediately in front of his feet to prevent him tripping over anything. He didn't want anyone to know he was out and about – even if they assumed it was to the toilet.

Now, when he thought he was about in the right place, he shone the torch briefly forward onto a small tent and breathed a sigh of relief to find it was the one that held the boxes of finds. He'd have to be very careful.

What seemed to him like an eternity later, he was hotter than he'd imagined possible – and no nearer to finding anything that caused the talisman even the slightest movement, let alone a real vibration.

Come on, Morris. What did you expect? There can't be that many slivers of ancient dragon vases waiting to be found. But somehow, he was disappointed. Taking off the lids, carefully checking each piece in the light of his torch, checking for an etched dragon tail or something similar – and fearing all the while that his movements or torchlight would wake someone up. Well, no wonder he was hot and bothered. It felt like a wild fool's errand and his temper was deteriorating with every boring piece of brown pottery he inspected.

Finally he pushed the lid back on the last box and straightened up, brushing his damp hair from his forehead and wondering why he felt so cross and frustrated. *I should be glad no one is taking dragon magic back to the town*, he thought guiltily. *If Scordril is right, someone bad might discover it and use it for evil.* And there *were* bad people in the world. They'd just fought a war about one of them.

———

Morris woke up with a start as Flick poked her head into his tent.

'You look as if you've had a bad night! Hurry up, lazybones. We have to get these tents down and packed up. Your mum asked if we'd had breakfast when I passed them just now.'

'Crumbs. What time is it?' he asked, shaking his head sleepily.

'Half eight, dopey! I'll light the fire.' And she pulled her head out and left him to get dressed.

It seemed only moments since he'd crawled into the tent, cold and damp and disheartened by what had seemed a complete waste of time, despite knowing how important it was to Scordil to safeguard ancient dragon property.

Later, scoffing a mountain of Weetabix in between mouthfuls of hot sweet tea, he looked up at Flick. 'You know what? I think we should ask if we can stay on for one more night.'

He was pleased to see the look of absolute delight and astonishment cross his cousin's face.

'You mean on our own?' she asked incredulously. 'That would be wonderful. But they'll never let us.'

'I think they will. There's going to be a full moon so it'll be light and safe – and who on earth would be wandering round here at night to attack us? If anywhere's safe, it's here.'

The truth was, he wanted some excitement after the failure to find another dragon shard. And if the dragons weren't going to supply it, then he and Flick had to supply their own. It would be fun to be alone, doing whatever they wanted. They could look out for each other fine – they weren't babies any more.

To their amazement, his mother hardly gave it a second thought.

'That's not a bad idea, Morris. We'll be very busy sorting everything out at home and you've still got lots of holiday. Yes, why not? It's only one night. Nothing much could go wrong in the rest of today and

145

overnight. You've managed fine so far. George, what do you think?' she asked, turning to Morris's father.

Morris's dad simply shrugged and said, 'Better drowned than duffers. If not duffers, won't drown. That's what the famous writer Arthur Ransome said – and anyway there's no lake so you won't drown!'

Morris looked puzzled. 'Does that mean yes?'

And it was arranged just like that. They were sent to the village to check with Flick's parents and when they arrived back breathless on site, there was no real camp any more. The cars were piled high with tents and boxes and luggage, a few adults were still wandering around, others were driving off slowly across the field to the gate. The two little tents that were left looked very lost and forlorn on their own.

Morris looked at Flick and grinned. 'Now for the fun,' he said under his breath.

CHAPTER 9

Blue Moon

*T*hey circled the bald patch of ground where the archaeologists had worked. The sticky air around Traprain and the humid afternoon were making Morris hot and irritable.

'Well, that's that,' he said, wiping his sweaty face with the back of his hand. 'We've looked in all the left-over holes, and walked everywhere and we haven't found anything.'

He just stopped himself from adding that his talisman hadn't picked up any dragonmagic, either, when he realised Flick wasn't to know about it.

He checked it was still in his pocket – presumably it would have vibrated, as Scordril had said, if he'd been near a piece of dragon pottery. With the adults gone and he and Flick having full run of the area around the Law, he'd hoped to find at least something good, even if not an ancient dragon artefact.

Flick stamped on a chunk of loose soil. 'I'm bored. Let's climb the steepest side of the Law.'

Morris raised his eyebrows. 'Are you mad? We'll melt…Oh all right, it might be fun to go up for the last time this holiday.'

'Great! Race you to that loose rock we found,' Flick yelled and darted away, leaving Morris to catch up, running as fast as the uneven ground would let him.

Scrambling and puffing, they reached the top of the Law, where Morris's father said King Loth had had his fort. They sagged to the ground, their backs to a rock. Morris was gasping for breath. Next to him, Flick fanned her face with her hand.

'One day we'll come back and shove this rock aside and see what's behind it,' she said. 'But right now, I don't think I could move a mouse.' She turned to stare over the fields at the dark clouds gathering. 'Look up there. Do you think we'll get soaked?'

'Probably.' Morris held out his hand to encourage a beetle to climb onto it. 'Just think: a storm brewing and us all alone up here!'

He squinted at the clouds and was surprised to see how fast they were moving in from the west. Swelling and tumbling over each other. *Now, that's odd*, he thought... but the sound of boots scraping on pebbles behind him cut across any further thoughts.

A woman appeared. 'Hello there. I followed you up. Good exercise, isn't it!'

Flick introduced her as Mrs Campbell from the post office. The woman perched herself on the ground beside them and discussed the likelihood of a storm while she shared the water from her canteen bottle.

Morris suddenly realised Flick wasn't listening. He nudged her.

She pointed to a group of birds swooping and fighting in the distance. 'Can you see those?'

148

Morris squinted. 'Magpies again! One, two... bother, there's too many to count.'

Mrs Campbell said quietly, 'Magpies gathering together are an ill omen.'

'Maybe it's the full moon tonight making them act up? You know, like it makes the tide high or low,' Morris said brightly.

But Mrs Campbell wasn't smiling. She seemed to have gone into a trance. 'Magpies flying near the window of a house foretell death.'

Morris shivered.

'Hello Mr Magpie, how's your wife?' Mrs Campbell said in a louder voice as the magpies flew nearer. 'My mother always said that, to avoid bringing disaster on us or our home.'

Morris thought the Campbell family sounded odd.

'Isn't it just the gathering storm that's disturbing them?' said Flick.

They stared at the birds. The magpies were circling around the Law now, their calls like the cackling laugh of a madman.

Mrs Campbell started counting them. '*One for sorrow, two for joy...*'

Morris and Flick joined in, '*Three for a girl and four for a boy,*' their voices growing to a crescendo. Getting to *Five for silver, six for gold*, everyone stopped counting and there was a sudden silence before Mrs Campbell spoke.

'There are seven, actually.'

Morris nodded. He could see perfectly well there were seven, and knew that it was *Seven for a secret never to be told* – but he didn't want to say anything. It was too close to home. He knew a secret that was so important he wanted to tell everyone – and it had to be kept hidden from all of them, even Flick.

He let his thoughts stray to the dragons, deep in their layr, below him, this very moment. He wondered what Scordril was doing…

Later, when Mrs Campbell had gone, Morris noticed that the clouds seemed to have settled down and only threatened rain in the far distance, over the North Sea.

Suddenly AT strolled up, tail aloft, as sure of himself as he had been when they first met him, and positioned himself with his back turned pointedly to Morris. Flick tickled AT on the top of his head and murmured once or twice to him. Morris was reminded of his visit inside the caves. He looked at the cat's patchy fur, messier than ever. *You've probably seen the dragons. Bet you could tell a tale or two*, he thought, realising he himself probably never would now.

Flick turned to him. 'I think I'll sleep like a log tonight. I'm so tired.' She pushed her face against the cat's coat and surprisingly he didn't resist. 'Anyway, we'd better head down for our tea. I'm famished.' Flick peered at Morris, around AT's head. 'Don't forget your mum left us that slab of cake. Coming?'

Morris nodded and followed Flick and AT, his mind running over the events of the last few days. He felt subdued. It was certainly the most eventful holiday he'd had. But it was over now and he couldn't talk to anyone about it.

Back at the tents, AT polished off a chunk of cake, then started to groom his whiskers.

Morris cleared away his tin plate. 'That cat isn't normal, eating cake like that!'

Flick yawned and smiled dreamily but made no attempt to defend AT. So Morris sat and thought of all the special things he might do to round off the holiday. In the end, he decided to do what he always did. 'I'm going to read for a while. And then I may take a look at the moon. Dad said there's a big one tonight.'

'You and your moon! Come on, AT. Help me wash up.'

The cat hissed alarmingly.

A few minutes later, they piled into their tents for the final night.

———◦◦◦———

Behind the clouds that formed and rolled over Traprain during the day, the dragons grouped into wings and flew in from Musselburgh for Njortin's celebration – everyone who had been involved in the rescue, plus a good many more who'd been selected by the drawing of sticks. All were eager to meet their newly found dragonkin, and of course to have a good time.

Those who arrived first brought food and helped with setting up the Great Chamber for the festivities. The layr was soon full of dragons scattering grass and twigs to make comfortable seats, stoking fires and preparing meat. Dragons met and talked over spitting and hissing flames, and the slop of water into drinking vessels.

When the time came to start, the mages from both layrs filed into the hall. Njortin led the way with Kvayn, Scordril and Thofirin behind them, then the others. There were roars and cheers. Njortin said a few words and then a dragonhorn rang through the chamber and the feasting started.

Time flew past and it was clear that the dragons from Traprain and Musselburgh were enjoying each other's company. After they had eaten, calls went up for a tale to be told. A proper dragon tale...

Scordril sent a picture of the shard on a tight mindlink to Kvayn with a query. He was still curious to know about the ancient artefacts and their power.

Kvayn nodded, sent the same query to Njortin, then rose and held up her claws.

»*I know of no finer storyteller than Njortin! I ask Njortin to step forward.*»

———⟨𝓋𝓋𝓋⟩———

Nodding his acknowledgement to Kvayn and the other mages, Njortin stood and turned away from the central gathering table. He shuffled forward slowly. His old bones, covered in their sagging scales, were stiff after sitting for so long. His stomach was full of juicy meat, and his tail dragged behind him like a lump of lead. The other dragons continued conversations behind him, or chewed noisily on the remnants of the banquet, as Njortin headed for the end of the hall, to the place allotted to storytellers – his favourite place in the whole layr. It was set against the deep blood-red wall, coloured by the ancestors and decorated with lustrous gold.

Njortin eased himself carefully onto the raised 'tale tellers' ledge and let his dark blue-grey body settle into a comfortable position. The mindspeech died down and an expectant hush fell over the hall.

Now he could see all the dragons ranged around makeshift tables of stone or wood, others crouched down around the walls. Their faces were turned towards him watching and waiting for him to speak. Eager faces were reflected in the glow from the flickering wall-torches. The youngones snickered, and poked at each other with their claws.

Njortin breathed deeply, licked his thin lips and began sending his deep, sonorous voice into the minds of every dragon, as he started telling the tale of Loth and Thenew.

»*Glows past, there was an overgrounder named Loth, a powerful overgrounder who ruled as king over others of his kind, and over all the lands around our layr. Over everywhere we hunted then and now. Even down to the sea itself. Lands that the overgrounders came to name Lothian after him. And he ruled from here at Traprain, living upon the very top of the Law, high above our heads...*«

Njortin raised his glittering dark green eyes and long snout to the roof; the younger dragons raised their snouts to the ceiling too, as if expecting to see Loth appear. The older dragons smiled as they watched the youngones.

Njortin glanced around his audience before continuing.

»Now Loth had a daughter, Thenew. With kindly eyes, the fairest of skin, their kin did say. Known for her gentleness to others and cleverness with herbs.»

As he spoke, Njortin felt his eyes drawn to where Threah sat beside Scordril at the central table.

»King Loth was a good king and a good overgrounder, brave and honest, but he was also proud. Too proud. For Thenew loved a shepherd and wanted to wed... to be his bonded life partner,» Njortin amended, as he saw the blank stares of the dragons who did not recognise the overgrounder term.

»So, Thenew came to her father and spoke of her love, but Loth would not agree. Undaunted, she begged him for consent until Loth became angry. His temper was fierce and swift to rise.»

As he spoke, Njortin saw Ygdrann turn to stare at Scordril and snort tiny flames of amusement. Scordril shuffled in his seat.

Sensing Scordril's discomfort and the possible reasons for it, Njortin swiftly pressed on. *»Loth roared and stamped, scattering his terrified watch-guards, as he spoke of utter disgrace, of the unsuitability of a lowly shepherd for the daughter of a king, of how his daughter should be punished. Thenew fell on her knees before him but to no avail. Loth had decreed it, so it would be – his shameful daughter should be thrown to her death from the summit of the Law!»*

There were gasps from the dragons nearby as Njortin stabbed the air with a gnarled claw. Many pairs of eyes flickered with silver lights of distress.

»Next glow, as the solar orb rose above the horizon,

Thenew was taken to the highest, steepest part of the Law. There was much grinding of teeth and wailing amongst the gathered overgrounders. So much grief that dragonkin could sense it in the layr. But Loth did not relent and she was thrown screaming over the edge to her death.»

Even the crackling fire-pit seemed to quieten as everyone in the Hall held their breath.

»But she did not die, no body was found…»

Njortin paused for a second.

»Her very own shepherd had summoned the other Traprain shepherds during the night and they in turn summoned dragons. For they knew our kind from dealings in the past. As she fell, Thenew tumbled down the Law, crashing from rock to branch amongst the gorse and elder shrub, and was snatched by a dragon at the very point of impact with the ground – a dragon who was disguised as a great elder bush and unseen by the overgrounders above.»

A young dragon over to Njortin's left sighed.

»The dragon carried her gently, concealed in his elder-bush wings, and passed her to the waiting shepherds who smuggled her overland, along secret herding paths to the sea, then by boat to Cuross. Dragons followed all the while, masked by trees and shrubs, as is still our custom. Thenew was badly injured in the fall and dragons used all their skill and knowledge of healing to help the shepherds nurse her. For a long time, she lived in Cuross with the shepherds, recovering. Protected by a dragonspell and wed – bonded – with her special shepherd.»

Njortin placed his claws on his knees and allowed

his shoulders to relax. His audience remained still, hypnotised by his voice.

»*Much later, Thenew returned to Traprain, bringing four bowls, worked by overgrounders from the finest local red earth. These she gave to the Traprain layr in gratitude. Rare artefacts indeed. They were used by the mages to perform the highest alchemy. My ancestor etched those bowls with his own claws. A different symbol on each so that they could be used for different purposes and their ingredients would never mix – a dragon head, a claw, a wing and a tail...*»

Njortin sensed the startled reaction of the Musselburgh mages, and nodded at Kvayn. The shard that saved Traprain and broke the dragongrid had almost certainly come from the bowl with the dragontail etching. Over time, it had – they had – become imbued with the very magic power they had come into contact with.

Sensing growing impatience to hear the rest of the story, Njortin continued. »*But to her dragon rescuer she gave the biggest honour. On return, she gave birth to a smallone, a male, and named him Kentigern after the dragon who kept her from death.*»

The air around Njortin rang with cries of delight. He held his claws up to signal he wasn't finished, but still he had to speak loudly across the clamour of mindspeech.

»*She continued her kindly ways to others, forgiving even those overgrounders who would throw her to her death. Even Loth himself, who by now regretted his cruel action. Her own kin named her St Enoch, which seemed a strange name...*»

Njortin clasped his claws together and proudly pushed out his snout. *»But we will always know her as a dragonfriend.»*

A loud rumble filled the Great Chamber and all eyes turned, startled, to Scordril. *»We may need many more dragonfriends if we are to survive the coming return of the nightdragons and their evil wingriders. We may be outnumbered and in grave peril. How many dragons are on watch duty tonight?»*

———✦✦✦———

It must have been long after midnight when Morris woke with a start. He found himself lying on his front on top of his open book, with his torch under his arm, its light flickering ominously. He quickly switched it off. How stupid to have fallen asleep with it on.

He twisted over and sat up. The inside of the tent glowed strangely, as if someone had drained all the colour from a photograph, including the blacks and whites. It was a transparent bluish light, almost ghostly – and then instantly he was wide awake.

Of course! This must be the full moon they'd promised, shining through the canvas. But what was the blue glow? In a flash he was out of his sleeping bag and pulling on an extra sweater and thick socks. Shoving his feet into his shoes, he fumbled for the tent door ties. The dew had soaked into them and he struggled to pull them undone, but finally he could see out into the field.

A ghoulish blue light covered the grass, the sky and

the distant trees, like a thin blanket that he could see through. Morris was just about to open his mouth and call for Flick when he shut it again. Some of the most wonderful things were best kept private. He'd enjoy it himself for a few minutes and then climb back into the warmth. Someone tomorrow would tell him what it all meant.

He crept further out and stood up, hugging himself to keep warm, slowly turning round to find the source of the light. A moth brushed against his face making him jump. He gazed around anxiously, half mesmerised by the eeriness of the experience and half afraid that someone would be there watching him.

But no, the site was as deserted as it had been when his parents left. The full moon shone through the slight mistiness up above him and off to the west – his neck hurt to stare constantly at that angle but he couldn't take his eyes off it. It was BLUE; not powder blue like icing on cakes and not bluish like the land around, but really blue. He gawped stupidly. How could it be?

He was just deciding that he had to tell Flick to look and take an interest, when something caught his attention in the corner of his eye. He whipped round and stared straight up at the clouds that were assembling into a mass of dark cotton wool to the north.

Between the cloud-shaped rain mass that darkened the northern sky, another shape flitted and wafted. His heart leapt. Was it a dragon? It was dark as night and sharply outlined by the patchy blueness around it. No. This was not Scordril or one of his friends. It was too…

jagged! This was something else. What had Scordril said about renegade dragons under the control of – what was the word? – *wingriders*, that was it! Riders who rode on the wings of dragons they'd captured – and he'd said they might come back! This must be one of them.

Fear gripped his chest so hard he thought he would never take another breath. What if it was a scout coming to see if it was time to kill the Traprain dragons? Morris didn't care if he got his pyjamas wet. He threw himself onto the ground and crawled as fast as he could back into the tent.

He rummaged desperately to find his shorts where the talisman lay, safely stuffed beside his hanky. Almost crying with relief as his hands closed round it, he screamed inside his head, 'Scordril!' – still seeing in his mind's eye the approaching dark shape – and heard with relief the immediate urgent reply in his head: »*I'm coming, overgrounder Morris. Stay where you are.*»

He sat very still for a long moment, shaken by the realisation of what he'd just done. When he'd stopped trembling, he crept outside again and called 'Flick' softly at the door of her tent. He wasn't sure what he was going to tell her but he needed her company. Not getting an answer, he untied the door and poked his head in.

In the unreal light from the moon, he saw that she was gone.

CHAPTER 10

Vanished

As soon as she'd been sure there was no more movement in Morris's tent next door, Flick had quietly pushed the dozy AT from where – surprisingly – he'd agreed to lie at the foot of her sleeping bag, and pulled on her jacket over her clothes.

There had been no point in getting undressed. With a full moon promised, this was the night to explore Hairy Craig on her own, since Morris was too scaredy-cat to accompany her. It was her only chance – she'd never be allowed to leave her own house at night and go exploring.

Flick picked up her torch and left the tent. AT had disappeared. She didn't dare call him. He'd turn up in due course. She wasn't kidded he was her friend – it simply suited him to stay with her from time to time. But she rather liked his company and found herself wishing he were hers – no one else would have such a large wild cat.

She was surprised to see that there was very little moonlight considering all the fuss about full moons. Just a faint glow from behind some thick mist. Better than nothing, but just as well she'd renewed her torch battery when they'd gone into the village.

'Which way?' she asked herself under her breath, and then resolutely set off across the field northwards, her footsteps padding oddly in the still night air. If she was going to have to use her torch for light, the quickest way would be most sensible.

She was half way round the western end of the Law when suddenly a strange gauzy blue lighted up the fields. She stopped dead, as shocked as if a police spotlight had picked her out committing a robbery. Whatever was happening?

She looked up to her right and noticed that the moon had come out from behind the mist – or rather the mist had withdrawn from the moon. What an amazing sight – it must be the moon Morris had gone on and on about – but he'd not said anything about blue. And he'd missed it while asleep!

She chortled to herself. What would he say when she told him?

This wicked thought sustained her all the way to Hairy Craig. If nothing else, it stopped her having to think about what she would do when she got there – because the truth was, she wasn't sure. She hoped she'd be brave enough to go in and take a look round. But the little disturbances in her stomach weren't all to do with hunger.

She wished AT were here, pushing his ragged fur aggressively against her legs. Anything rather than absolute silence in this unearthly glow.

'Ow!' she shrieked in fear as something hurtled into her leg. She looked down. AT stood there, back arched, tail wagging loftily from side to side and a look on his face that clearly said, 'You can't do this without me. You'd be scared.'

'You wretched—' she began, and then laughed shakily. 'Okay. You're coming too. Well, you know the tunnels better than I do, so maybe it's a good idea.'

She could have sworn he grinned a 'told you so' reply before setting off into the cave they'd found the other day.

She took a deep breath and followed him – but not before looking carefully at the moon to estimate how long she had before it would set. She'd be finished if her battery ran out and the moon disappeared before she was back at the campsite.

—◆◇◆—

Flick was losing her sense of direction in the tunnels. *Not quite lost*, she told herself without wholly believing it, and shivered. There was a definite cool breeze. How odd… *But a draught means a way out, surely?* she thought, concentrating now on the place up ahead where the tunnel split, yet again. She didn't want to go further without AT's guidance.

'I bet you know the way in and out!' she said, turning to AT, who had been running ahead and then lagging behind as if checking they were alone. He wasn't in front.

He's very quiet. Where's he gone? She flashed her torch back up the tunnel. There was absolutely no sign of him. 'AT…A…T…!' Flick yelled back up the way they'd come, and the dull echo rang around the rocky walls and her head.

Fed up with his games, she picked up a chunk of rock and chucked it at a dark corner. A piece of the shadow separated itself and darted out – followed by the clatter of a landslide of rocks and a strangled yowl.

Her heart lurched and she darted forwards – and almost trod on AT. She bent over him in dismay.

He lay on the tunnel floor, surrounded by rocks and blood. One of his eyes flickered open and stared up at her briefly before closing. Then he began a low, dreadful rattling hiss through his teeth, his tongue sticking out to one side.

In the wobbly beam from her torch Flick saw that the cat's head was a mess of torn fur and blood. A trickle of blood was running onto the ground in a horrible dark pool.

'Oh heck.' Flick crouched beside him and gently touched the cat's side. AT winced. Panic rose in Flick's throat and she blinked back an urge to cry.

Angrily pulling herself together, she considered the stricken cat. AT's breathing sounded bad. 'I can't move you. I daren't touch you! What if it makes you worse?' she whispered.

The worst was that AT could die.

She struggled to remove her jacket and laid it over the cat, making soothing noises. 'I'll stay with you. I won't leave,' she promised, wondering what she could possibly do, so far from help.

AT didn't move. He hardly seemed to breathe.

Flick hoped Morris would eventually miss her and

get a search party together. But who and when? *When his parents come back, to collect us, that's when. But that's too long...* She huddled up next to AT, willing him to hang on.

The moon will have set by now, Flick thought miserably a short time later. She'd turned off her torch to save the batteries, switching it on from time to time to check on AT. He now lay still, though she could feel the gentle movement of his chest. The blood was drying on his fur.

'AT?' she said.

There was no response, but she had the strange feeling his head had shifted just a fraction since she'd last looked. He seemed to have turned towards the place where the tunnels split and held his position, as if in a trance. His lips were drawn back over his teeth and his ears flattened – almost as if he were watching a mouse.

Then the huge wild cat let out a long drawn-out miaow. A strange, low sound, so quiet it seemed to run off into a hiss as it disappeared down the distant dark tunnels.

'What's the matter? What—?' Was he going to die on her just like that?

AT repeated the low hiss.

Shortly after, Flick heard another faint sound. A strange leathery flapping and scuffling came from the direction AT faced. The hairs on Flick's bare arms stood on end as if a chill wind had blown up. Her hands shook so violently that they switched off the torch. Her teeth chattered, and blood pounded in her ears. Then she made out footsteps – scraping, heavy footsteps.

AT's eerie mewling still hung on the air. Flick clutched at the furry body for comfort, watching for anything moving in the darkness.

Then a tongue of flame shot out, trembling through the blackness for a moment, a single orange and silver flash, like a fire-breather at the circus. Reflected in the light, she saw eyes, narrow green eyes staring towards her and AT. Her heart leapt up to her throat strangling any scream.

Next instant, she felt a warm breath beside her.

Fire... Wild animals are afraid of fire.

She had no fire, but she had a torch. Her quaking hands snapped on the light.

The cat's eyes were wide open now – and next to his face was another: a broad, dark blue, scaly snout, teeth like she couldn't imagine on any beast she knew, and the green eyes. The head with the snout reared back and claws came up to protect the face. A pair of wings, like a giant bat thrust out...

Then it was gone, vanished in a sparkle of lights, dancing across her vision and shrinking to the size of a normal head, a man's face.

And a normal pair of hands held up a lighted firebrand, casting pools of brightness around them.

'Ah, who is here... Are you hurt like my friend?' The man's voice was deep and powerful. It sounded foreign.

Flick fought the urge to gabble all her words at once and just shook her head dumbly, staring. Was she mad? Where had the monster gone?

But the stranger's dark face smiled back, a strange smile. Ordinary, greenish eyes were gazing at Flick.

'Here, overgrounder… I mean here, hold this.' The man thrust the burning wood into Flick's free hand. 'Straag needs help.'

Then he turned away, leaving Flick holding the burning firebrand, and started to tend to AT. One hand ran over the outline of the cat, and the man began to murmur words, bizarre words, or so it sounded to Flick, like so much gobbledegook. The other hand rested on AT's head.

Flick switched off her own torch and watched in silence. *Hunger: that must be it, hunger and the worry*, she thought as she watched the stranger. *Otherwise I'd understand his words.*

A crackling noise, like leaves blowing along the ground in a wind, rushed towards the huddled group, along the tunnel. A glow seemed to form around the stranger as he spoke. The words blurred together again and Flick felt slightly dizzy as if the tunnel were spinning round her.

AT twitched and stirred.

The stranger, his hair blowing around his head for a moment, raised his hands up, away from AT…The air filled with tiny sparkling lights, then vanished. The stranger stood back, and turned to stare at Flick.

She rubbed her eyes. The man seemed to have finished something. But she wasn't sure what.

But it felt safe now to ask questions. Her voice came out wobbly.

'You called him Straag. Who are you? And how did you know we were here?'

'Straag is my friend. He called and I came.' The man

looked at her closely. 'Who are *you* and why are you here with Straag?'

'Flick.' She paused. 'I was exploring with AT…that's what we call Straag. He got himself hurt when those rocks fell.' She squirmed. She felt partly responsible for AT's injury.

The man took back his fire-torch from Flick. 'Flick, eh?'

Flick looked at AT, who appeared to be breathing normally now.

The stranger also looked down at AT. 'Straag is better.'

Amazingly, as if to emphasise it, AT rose to his feet with great dignity, staggered slightly, miaowed a single tuneless sound and then ran swiftly away into the shadows without a backward glance.

Flick gaped in disbelief, and turned back to stare at the man.

'But…he was very badly hurt… How did—?' she began, but the man simply stared back, his eyes sparkling in the flames of his torch's shifting light.

Flick felt she was going mad. How could she have mistaken AT's injuries; surely he'd been nearly dead?

'I am…trained in these things,' the man said and bent to pick up Flick's jacket and hand it to her.

'Thanks. You never said who you are. Or where you came from.'

Doubts were beginning to form in her mind. 'Is that the way out? I really must get back…to my friend.'

She suddenly felt very frightened. She reached down and picked up her torch.

The green eyes twinkled in the eerie light from the

flames. 'You are safe with me, Flick. I am Jarl… Jarl.' His lips pulled back and the smile became a contorted grin.

———◦◦◦———

Morris stared at the empty sleeping bag. Where was Flick? She couldn't be in the toilet tent because his father had dismantled it and dug them a small hole nearer to their tents, behind a bush, leaving them the pile of dirt to fill it in with.

His hand clutched the talisman. He could still hear Scordril's voice in his mind. He would so like to know how it was possible to have called him with the talisman and got an answer.

But he was frightened to death of the thing in the sky. He glanced up again. It was difficult to make out if it was still there among the black clouds. Maybe he'd imagined it? Brought Scordril out in vain? The blue hue that hung over the field had faded – the moon was rapidly disappearing behind misty clouds as it slowly moved towards the western horizon, and from the east a tiny thin line of pre-dawn false light – as his father called it – was casting a different dim glow over the tents.

A flapping behind him made him swing round in fear. He trembled so badly he had to grab the tent pole to keep his balance. A dragon was landing just yards from where he stood. The scream died in his mouth as he realised this was not a black dragon but—

'Scordril!' he exclaimed, not caring who heard. They were alone anyway.

»*Sorry I scared you,*» Scordril said quickly. »*I didn't have time to walk over like a meandering overgrounder—*»

'She's gone, Flick's disappeared!' Morris blurted out, then realised what had just happened. 'You spoke without speaking again. How did you do it?'

'I don't think we have time to discuss mindspeech right now, Morris – remind me later,' said Scordril, changing instantly into Roderick. 'I'll teach you how. But Flick – where is she? And how long was the nightdragon here before you called me?'

'I don't know where she is… I don't know anything! I looked in the tent and she wasn't there… I only looked in after I called you. I wanted to show her the blue moon.'

'Blue moon?'

'It doesn't matter. But it was only a minute or two after I'd seen the…thing in the sky. I knew it wasn't one of your friends. This one was too long, and thinner and very black, and anyway you wouldn't have been up there among the black clouds. You said about—?' He was blabbing.

'Yes, nightdragons. They'll be coming soon. That was one of their scouts I saw in your mind. We've wasted too much time. Get a coat or something. We have to find Flick. Tell me where you think she might be.'

Morris felt something like panic rising in his chest. He couldn't think. Too much was happening at once. He wanted to run away. 'I don't know,' he said again. 'I can't think.'

'Then get your coat – and I'll help you think.'

Morris pushed into his tent and pulled his jacket on over his jumper. No point in changing from his pyjamas now. He didn't even know what Scordril was planning. But just as he fastened the buttons, a strange warmth filled his mind and he felt a calmness flowing from the tip of his head to his stomach. He felt the muscles unlock and fall back into place – and suddenly he knew where Flick was.

'Hairy Craig,' he shouted. He was doing a lot of shouting tonight but he didn't care. 'That's where she'll be – she wanted to explore it,' he told Scordril as he emerged from the tent.

'Hairy Craig?'

Bother, he'd forgotten the dragons wouldn't call it Hairy Craig.

'It's a rocky outcrop–'

»*Show me!*»

Roderick was speaking right into his head again. Morris looked into his eyes and thought of where Hairy Craig was. But how was he to tell Scordril?

»*Got it!*» said Roderick, almost growling in his urgency. »*Now, go behind me and hold round my neck. That's right, like that. Tight!*»

'But—'

Before he could protest, Morris was surrounded by two enormous leathery dark wings that flapped up a storm around him. He found himself rising from the ground on the back of Scordril's long scaly neck. His arms could no longer cross now that it was a dragon neck he clung to, so he hung on by interlocking all his fingers and squeezing them till his arms ached from the effort.

Buffeted this way and that, he felt sick with fear – and excitement. He'd wanted to see a dragon and now he was riding one.

»*We have a tiny hole of time, much less than half a glow, to find your cousin and bring her to safety before the wingriders attack.*»

»*But she'll see you!*» Morris tried thinking to Scordril. It was totally impossible to talk over the noise of the wings and the wind. He hoped his message would get through but he didn't know how to do it properly.

»*Flick may have to see me if we are to save her, but no other overgrounders will. The night is deserted. No one will come out now. You have seen the rain clouds?*»

Morris had – and spatters of rain were falling on him as he clung onto Scordril. He hoped he wasn't throttling him. He hoped the neck scales wouldn't get slippery and make him lose his arm-and-knee grip. He didn't want to swivel round and hang under Scordril as he flew!

Terror began to claw at his mind.

In an effort to stem the fear, he stared into the darkness as they flew. Scordril circled, higher and higher, and then flew off towards the north. Morris could make out the lights from some boats at anchor in the Forth, much further away than Hairy Craig.

»*The entrance is this side,*» he 'thought' at Scordril again.

»*I know,*» said Scordril, surprising him. »*There was a tunnel mentioned when I read the Chronicles.*»

»*That'll be where Flick is,*» Morris replied gloomily, shivering as he remembered his own narrow escape. »*She'll have got lost.*»

»*Just like you did?*»

»*How d'you know that?*» Morris demanded.

»*You sent the picture and the fear in your thoughts as you spoke,*» said Scordril in the nearest thing to a dragon laugh that Morris could imagine.

»*Hold on now!*» Scordril said, suddenly serious again – and Morris realised he'd probably been talking to distract him from the terror of flying. If he could sense what was in his mind, he'd have known about that, too. Somehow, it felt comforting. Maybe they'd find Flick and get to safety in time.

But instantly another thought struck him, leaving his senses reeling. If she'd met a dragon in the tunnel she might already be dead.

CHAPTER 11

The Battle

As Scordril flew in to land on the south side of Hairy Craig, the distant view of the Forth disappeared from sight, leaving only the faintest of pre-dawn light, already partly obscured by light rain clouds.

A moving dark shadow slipped creepily around the rocks at the entrance to the cave.

Morris started. He was about to warn Scordril of danger when the great dragon landed with a spine-shaking jolt and folded his wings. At that moment, the shape rushed towards Morris and he screamed.

In an instant he found himself clinging to Roderick's neck, from behind, as he had when they started out. Feeling stupid because he'd screamed and because he was hanging onto a man's neck, he quickly dropped down, glad of the covering gloom, and found himself tangled up in AT. The enormous feral cat was hissing and spitting, pushing between Morris's legs as he sniffed around him.

'You stupid oaf,' he shouted angrily.

Roderick turned round. 'Straag! I might have known... But come on, youngone, we need to hurry.'

Morris ran to catch up as the overground version of Scordril strode towards the cave entrance.

'How do you mean "Straag"? Do you know—? ...Scordril! Look!' His voice ended up strangled in a hoarse whisper as he stared, transfixed, at the sky.

Scordril turned and looked upward past the dark jagged outline of the cave.

A large group of black dragons – the so-called nightdragons – was pouring in from the east. So close they could make out the shapes of the two wingriders sitting astride the sharply indented wings of the leading dragons. The air was filled with a distant rumble, like a fading thunderstorm – except that this storm was approaching and far more dangerous than any natural one. Morris felt the hairs on his neck rise.

He looked at Scordril in terror. 'Should we tell them? Warn them?'

'We have watchdragons – and our own magic barrier now. No one can get through unnoticed.'

Morris grabbed Scordril's sleeve. 'Then why fight at all? Why risk your friends? Why not wait inside for them to go away again?'

Scordril strode into the cave, ignoring Morris's questions. 'Come on, hurry! Flick and you are in danger here.'

—◦◦◦—

Scordril knew he could see inside the cave far better than the boy could, so he waited a moment for Morris's eyes to adjust before setting off towards the tunnel at the far end.

He could make himself small enough to walk through the tunnel if he reverted to dragon form, but he didn't want to frighten the children. Morris himself had only just seen him as a dragon for the first time since that day when Flick had fallen over the cliff. The girl would probably die of shock if she came face to face with one. So he had to remain in human form.

He walked into the tunnel that Morris had already discovered and where the boy suspected Flick was now trapped. Overgrounders! Sometimes they were more harm than help, he thought crossly.

Then he remembered how Morris had kept his secret, had lent him the fragment of pottery, had cared about what happened to them as if they were friends. And how they, too, were now in danger when they might have gone home with their parents if he hadn't made friends with him. He quickened his pace.

»*The nightdragons would just come back,*» he said, hoping the boy would remember what he'd asked. »*We need to sort this evil out now, before something worse happens to dragonkind and we cease to exist.*»

The boy didn't answer. Maybe he couldn't reliably do it yet.

'We need to mindspeak in here,' Scordril whispered to Morris. 'You can do it whenever you want, because of the talisman I gave you. I do not know what to expect in here. And I do not want to frighten Flick if she is alone.'

»*That's okay,*» came the voice in his mind. »*But I'll*

175

just hold on to your jacket, if you don't mind. I don't think I want to get lost again. I just wanted to see a dragon when I came before.»

Scordril nodded. »*An inquisitive youngone brings disaster, we say.*»

He sensed Morris wondering if it was he or Flick who had brought disaster. »*But also wealth, sometimes,*» he added kindly. »*A wealth of friendship and help.*»

Scordril stopped suddenly. They had rounded a corner in the wide passageway where it grew narrower. There was a rock fall up ahead. He knew Morris couldn't see it, but with dragonsight it was clear. And there was something else further along.

He reached out a hand to Morris to stop him pushing past. »*Morris, there is a dragon somewhere up ahead. I do not yet know who it is. Stay very close behind me. I can also scent Flick. I am not sure how she is. It is very faint.*»

Better to forewarn the youngone, he thought grimly as they moved along, their feet shuffling on the gravel.

Fifty yards more and he stopped again, rigid with shock. »*Jarl!*» he snarled at the crouching form of the dark blue dragon. »*What have you done to the overground youngone?*»

Behind him, he heard Morris gasp and instinctively put an arm back to hold him motionless. Then he slowly morphed into his true form, dwarfing Jarl deliberately into submission as his mage power manifested itself to the other dragon's mind, and let out a steady but harmless stream of fire into the air.

In the red, orange and yellow light waving gently round the rocky walls of the passageway, they could see quite clearly the slim form of Flick curled up on the floor at Jarl's feet, unmoving.

»*She is sleeping,*« said Jarl simply. »*Did you think I would kill her? She has been telling me of her home, her cousin – who I presume is this overgrounder boy with you? – and how she wanted to explore and find some treasure. I have admitted I am a dragon since she had already seen me as I arrived to help Straag, not knowing she was here. Now she will not be frightened when she wakes.*«

»*There is no time to lose,*« growled Scordril, knowing he was angry with relief rather than from bad temper. Though Threah would dispute that. He turned to Morris. 'Wake your cousin quickly.'

To Jarl he said, »*Why have you not led her out? Well, no matter, we must all go now. We must take them to safety. The nightdragons are gathering.*«

Scordril felt Morris shiver against him, having overheard the mindspeech. Overgrounders were not used to battle in the skies unless it was with aeroplanes and wars. 'Do not be afraid, youngone. We will get you to your tent where we will protect you both.' He spoke out loud for Flick's sake.

Morris pushed her roughly and she woke, struggling to sit up.

'Jarl?' she said, without flinching at the dragon towering above her. 'Where is AT? I mean, Straag? Morris, you came! And—?'

'It's Roderick,' said Morris. 'He's really called Scordril. So you've found out about dragons and you're not afraid!

I'm glad. I hated keeping secrets. We can talk about it – but there's going to be a dragon war or something. It's awful. We have to get away.' He pulled her to her feet.

At that moment AT strolled into the pool of light and swiped his tail against Flick. She hugged him but he snarled indignantly and pulled himself free.

Scordril touched Jarl's mind and received a full picture of what had happened in the tunnel.

»*I did not move the overground girl because I knew there was danger outside,*» said Jarl, »*So we talked about dragons and overgrounders and our history of helping each other in the past, and I was wondering what was best to do next when she simply fell asleep. I believe it is her night time.*»

Scordril mentally noted that Jarl had been thinking instead of acting impetuously – and then, feeling suddenly ashamed of himself, realised how he had immediately assumed Jarl had harmed the girl. He sent a feeling of remorse to Jarl and started outlining his plan in overground tongue.

'Both of you know we are dragons, so we are going to take you to the tents on dragonback. It is the only way to beat the wingriders' arrival – if indeed it is not already too late.'

He mindspoke with Straag, and immediately the feral cat loped his way back through the tunnel, past the dividing of the ways, unerringly taking the correct path to Hairy Craig, as Morris had called it. He and Jarl followed swiftly behind Morris and Flick. Scordril shared with Jarl the few things he didn't now know. He then checked what Njortin, Theofin and the others had done since he'd rushed out of the feast, leaving them with his mental image of the terrified boy and the nightdragon scout.

At the cave entrance, the children paused for breath but both he and Jarl moved outside and, in a flash, morphed to their full size for flight. The Law, under the near dark sky of high summer, was alive with black shapes and flashes of light. He glanced piercingly at Jarl. Yes, he was sure he could trust him now. But would the other dragons?

Scordril turned his head towards Morris and Flick in the cave entrance, lowered his forearms to the ground and tilted one wing to the ground like a slide.

»*Tell Flick that you are both to climb up a wing and hang on to our necks. Jarl will carry Flick. Quickly now! Tell her as well that she will not be able to hear us while we fly but that we will be talking to you.*«

He didn't add that over the Law the battle had started. When the children emerged from the cave, they would realise all too soon, and their fear would prevent them listening to further instructions.

———◦/◦/◦———

Morris gasped as Scordril rose from the ground at a steep angle, not circling to gain height but moving sideways to allow Jarl to take off. Within moments, they were as high as the Law. What he saw made him shiver with fear.

Many dark shapes dipped and swooped over the flat top. Fire flamed as dragon attempted to torch dragon. Morris saw two dragons fall to the ground as the fire hit them. He screamed. He had no way of knowing who was on whose side. He shut his eyes and clung to Scordril's neck, arms aching with tension.

When he next opened his eyes, he saw a wingrider fall off his dragon – even at this distance his shriek sounded like torture in Morris's head, mixed with the keening of the nightdragons who presumably had lost their riders. Or maybe it was a battle cry. He couldn't tell. He wished he could see Flick, but she was somewhere behind him on Jarl.

Smoke and fire rose now from the Law. It was still too dark to make out a pattern or a plan to the attack and defence. The nightdragons were sharper in outline and their snouts were more stubby, but they were moving so fast that it became a blur to Morris and he just hoped that the Traprain Law dragons were in amongst them somewhere, defending their territory and their loved ones. He felt an excited violence rise up in his stomach. He actually wanted them to be numerous and powerful and to slaughter the enemy wholesale.

Then he heard the cry, »*Yorheim!*« in his head.

He stared. What or who was 'Yorheim'?

Scordril was not sending him any speech but he suddenly changed direction with a jerk that made Morris clamp his legs even tighter to the neck and swung in towards the Law. Towards the centre of the fighting.

Jarl, too, had turned as one with Scordril and was now on his left.

—◦◦◦—

Scordril's anger knew no bounds as he saw Yorheim – that quiet, friendly steady beast – being attacked from all sides by three nightdragons. And six wingriders intent on harming him, urging on their stupid dragonmounts with strange calls and words. That made nine to one! By dragonclaws, an unfair fight.

»*Brygnon!*« he sent urgently, seeing the strong and sturdy watchdragon turn away from eliminating a smaller nightdragon. »*Yorheim needs help!*«

But even as he issued the command, a larger evil-looking nightdragon launched an attack on Brygnon and the watchdragon had to turn back to defend himself.

Jarl was pouring a torrent of flame at the first of Yorheim's attackers. One of the animal's wings flew off, severed at the chest, and passed so close to Scordril's head that he felt Morris duck on his back.

»*Just hold tight, Morris,*« he sent to the youngone. The de-winged dragon fell instantly to his death. He hoped it wouldn't be his own fate in an unguarded moment. He couldn't imagine what would happen to the overground youngone if that happened.

Scordil dived suddenly under the nightdragon who was tormenting Yorheim from behind. He knew this put Morris at even greater risk, but he only needed a second to do what he had in mind. And the sooner this was over, the better.

Quickly, he threw his head back and poured flame upward in a searing streak of lightning, right across the underbelly of the dragon. It shuddered violently as if it would burst under the enormity of the pain it felt. Its two riders lost their grip and fell screaming to the ground far below.

The nightdragon turned tail and disappeared into the skies. So! The way to win this battle was to injure the wingriders. Once out of their riders' control, their mounts had no will to fight.

Scordril sent an urgent order on a wide link to any of his kin who might hear him, hoping that only the Traprain dragons would understand the words.

Yorheim was bleeding heavily from a clawed back leg, and one wing had a tear to its edge. Catching sight of Ennasif butting and fending off an older gnarled nightdragon over to his right, Scordril's anger rose. No beast was going to be allowed to put an end to the friendship that had just started between the two layrs – the fact that Ennasif had taken a liking to Yorheim was something that would reunite the futures of the two layrs. It was worth fighting for.

But Yorheim was in no state now to defend himself.

»*Now!*« Scordril mindspoke to Jarl, and the two of them swooped, as one, at the third dragon who was attacking Yorheim's undamaged wing.

Before Scordril could act, Jarl torched the nightdragon with a blast so strong that even Scordril closed his inner eyelid to protect himself from it. He watched as the nightdragon turned into scorched flesh and fell out of the sky. There was nothing to be seen of the wingriders, who moments before had been whooping triumphantly. Yorheim was safe.

At the same moment, Yorheim sank slowly to the ground below the standing stones. He sat trembling as

Jarl and Scordril, with their young charges, joined him. They had shelter for no more than a moment.

A voice in Scordril's head spoke. »*We know a way into the layr where Yorheim can go to be safe. Flick found it. It's on the other slope... I'll show you.*»

Scordril turned his neck towards Morris. »*You already have, youngone. I can read the image.*»

Jarl turned to Morris. »*Me too! That way has not been opened for so long I had forgotten all about it. Not since Brekk*—» He broke off.

But Scordril said, »*Morris, tell Flick to get off Jarl and mount up behind you on me. Hurry!*» He lowered his wing as Morris conveyed the instructions to his cousin.

Then he said, »*Jarl, assist Yorheim back to that tunnel. The ground falls away steeply here, so he will only need a little help to fly without having to raise himself up. Get him to safety. You did well!*»

»*This is where I rescued Flick from the ledge!*» Scordril added inconsequentially to Morris as he took off again, this time with twice the burden.

———⟨o/o/o⟩———

Within moments they were back at their tents and Scordril was Roderick once more. Morris looked at Flick and both of them grinned sheepishly. They were ragged, cold and very jittery.

They could barely hear the battle up on the Law and Morris felt that the tents looked so ordinary sitting there in the growing dawn that they might have dreamt it all. He was dog-tired. Flick looked all in.

'When our smallones are tired and frightened we tell them to sleep in the firepit together – when the flames are out, of course!' said Scordril. 'But you are not smallones and not frightened…'

Morris looked at Flick. There was no one here to jeer at them. A silent agreement passed between them. 'That is a very good idea, Roder— I mean, Scordril,' he said out loud.

Flick quickly pulled her sleeping bag into Morris's tent while Scordril waited, tapping his feet on the dew-covered grass and glancing from time to time up at the hill above them.

When they were both safe inside their sleeping bags, Scordril said, 'Hold your talisman, Morris. I will need to morph now, but I will use the talisman to weave a spell round this tent till daylight comes. If you hold the talisman and stay inside, you will be safe. No dragon will be able to see you. You can talk about your adventures!'

'We won't move,' said Morris shakily. 'Are you going back to the battle?'

There was no answer, but a yellowy-red glow travelled round the tent on the inside, and a flapping of wings and wind told him Scordril had gone to help see off the rest of the enemy.

He turned to say something to Flick but she was already fast asleep. He was just about to close his eyes, clutching the talisman inside his hand, when he heard Scordril's voice once more, faint but clear.

»*Only till glowbreak. I shall come for you then.*»

184

CHAPTER 12

Talismans

Morris woke with a start. He realised he was still dressed. Faint early morning light was filtering around the half-closed tent flap. He listened for any noise outside, but all he could hear was the sound of Flick snoring, as she lay huddled in her sleeping bag next to him.

In a rush, the events of last night flooded back. Sweating, he sat up, frantically searching in his sleeping bag for the talisman. Only when he was clutching the smooth shape, cold, like a pebble straight from the sea, did he know it wasn't a dream.

His shuffling disturbed Flick.

'What…who?' Flick mumbled, squinting up at him. She raised herself up on one elbow.

'Morning, we'd better get up…quick. Scordril said he was coming.' Morris hastily tried to crawl from his bedding. As he was fighting within the cramped space he heard a loud noise outside. The tent shivered and a yellowy glow spun across the canvas before disappearing in a flash. Flick shook her head as if to get the sleep out of her eyes.

Scordril's voice spoke clearly and urgently into

Morris's mind. »*Morris, you are both safe, I trust? May I enter the tent?*»

»*Yes, no… We're awake and decent, I mean… Hang on a minute.*» Turning to Flick, Morris said, 'Scordril's here.'

Before either of them could say more, the tent flap was thrown aside and Scordril, or rather the overgrounder face of Roderick, pushed through. Scordril crammed himself into the tent and crouched down next to the two children. 'There are no other overgrounders here, yet?'

Morris thought that Scordril's face looked tired and drawn. Trying to straighten his crumpled clothes and drag a jumper over the top, he said, 'No… My parents aren't coming to take us home until this afternoon.'

Flick was sitting up now, too. 'And we haven't had anything to eat yet,' she added.

Scordril smiled, 'You can eat in a while, Flick. First, I am here to take you to the others. Njortin wishes to meet you. The dragons are assembled in the Great Hall in Traprain layr.'

'Meet us?' Morris gaped. 'Meet the other dragons?'

'Njortin?' Flick said.

'Njortin is dragonmaster at Traprain. He wishes to speak with you – as his honoured guests.' Scordril started to leave.

'We… we didn't dream it, did we?' Morris said, suddenly doubting everything. 'There was a battle here last night, wasn't there?'

'Yes, there was, and it is over,' called Scordril over his shoulder.

He waited until the others followed and they all stood in front of the tent, everyone looking slightly bedraggled.

Flick looked distressed and reaching out a hand to touch Scordril's arm, 'Is everyone, did anyone…?'

'We lost three good dragons.' Scordril seemed to stoop with the weight of his words. 'Braugnir, Minikk and Kyrekk… I have come from our service of remembrance, and casting their ashes to the winds above the Forth.'

Morris shivered and whispered, 'The nightdragons?'

'All destroyed. Their evil wingriders, too. They will not return to enslave our kin.' Scordril turned and strode a few paces forward, beckoning the others to follow.

Flick didn't move. Morris saw her blanch and his stomach turned.

Scordril had stopped, and was waiting, turning his head this way and that and sniffing the air. 'It is too far to walk. I will carry you on my back. You remember how to do that? I will show you what it is to ride in the air when there is no danger.'

With that, the overgrounder Roderick simply fell away into nothingness. A sparkle of lights dazzled Morris's eyes as the human shape was replaced by Scordril, tall and proud in his dragon form. He stood before Flick and Morris, the bronze brown of his scales glinting dully in the early sunlight. His chocolate veined wings were spread wide and he flapped them two or three times. He stared at the children with eyes that seemed to change constantly between gold and green. It was the first time that either Morris or Flick had seen a dragon close up in broad daylight, with no danger around. Still, Morris felt his heart pounding.

»*Morris, help Flick up first, then you,*« Morris heard Scordril say.

He did as he was asked and then felt the air rushing about Flick and him as Scordril thrashed his wings back and forward and rose from the ground.

A swirling mist gathered around the group as they became airborn. Startled, Morris realised it was forming into a cloud as they climbed higher and higher. He could see above and below Scordril but the cloud enveloped the edges of his wings. Morris heard Flick shriek with laughter, but the sound was immediately whisked away by the air. The cloud moved with them. »*Scordril, is this magic?*« he yelled in his mind.

»*Youngone! Speak quietly in your mind, otherwise I shall have a headpain!*«

Scordril checked his flight and circled the Law, as if providing his passengers with an eagle-eye view of the area. »*We are protected by a magecloud. Overgrounders will not see us. This is how we travel by day... Hold fast!*«

It was only a few moments in the air, but Morris knew he would remember it as clearly as if it had been longer. Too soon, they were back on solid ground outside the main entrance to the layr. He let himself be guided by Scordril through the opening, which appeared out of the scrubby hillside. With Flick, he was ushered down a tunnel. But this wasn't like the small tunnels at Hairy Craig. This was how he'd imagined a layr entrance would be, ever since he'd known that dragons lived at Traprain. Torches burned on the walls here and there, like they did in the stories of medieval knights' castles.

They only saw two dragons as they walked. Watchdragons, Scordril said. The dragons bowed their snouts and stared at Morris and Flick with a look of curiosity as they passed. Flick stared back and tripped over Scordril's tail, twice, before he altered his position to walk between the children so his tail dragged along the ground behind them.

The group stopped in front of a pair of wooden doors. Huge heavy-looking things, with figures of dragons set into the wood. Red jewels glistened where the eyes would be. Morris sensed something in his mind, but it sounded strange, a mournful, keening noise like thousands of seagulls all calling into the wind at once. The sound stopped as Scordril raised his claws and pushed the doors apart.

For a second or two, Morris felt that his whole body would explode with sheer wonder and excitement. In front of him was a vast hall full of torches, glinting on dragon scales. There were more dragons than he ever thought possible in one place. They parted and let their guests enter.

Ahead of him there was a pit, a gigantic campfire, burning and throwing out heat. They walked across the richly coloured floor, nodding to the dragons, as they in turn bowed their snouts to the overgrounders. At the far side of the hall a separate group of dragons – important dragons, Morris guessed – had arranged themselves below three torches set on the wall behind them. The wall glistened gold and dark red.

The dragons stood and waited. Scordril said to Morris, »*Tell Flick to do as you do...she will understand us soon enough.*» Morris whispered this instruction to Flick and she turned to him, wide-eyed, her red-blond curls glowing in the torchlight, and nodded.

Then one of the three dragons, who looked very old to Morris, with a snout that was wrinkled with age, stepped forward. For some reason Morris felt as if the headmaster was calling him to the front in assembly.

»*Njortin, mage and dragonmaster of Traprain, these are the overgrounder youngones, Morris and Flick,*» Scordril said to the dragon.

The elderly dragon, Njortin, dipped his long snout forward and then inspected the children with his glittering dark green eyes. His lips pulled back from his worn teeth. Flick hadn't heard a word of course, and Morris noticed her quizzical look at Scordril and then Njortin. Morris stepped forward and looked up at Njortin. Flick followed.

»*We're pleased to meet you, sir...but my cousin Flick doesn't understand mindspeech yet.*» Morris sensed all the dragons around were amazed by an overgrounder speaking with the highest of the dragons. He gulped. Had he done wrong?

»*Welcome, overgrounder Morris. I thank you on behalf of the Lothian dragons for your help. Without your precious gift of a part of our ancestors' shard we would not have woven a spell in time to save ourselves. For this, Scordril gave you the talisman.*»

Morris drew the dragon gift out of his pocket and held it out. Njortin nodded.

»*With the talisman you warned us of the nightdragon scout. We are in your debt. Now—*» Njortin turned to face Flick and held his claws out. They contained a smooth, pebble-shaped stone, like Morris's but darker in colour, more reddish, almost coppery. Morris pointed to the stone and told Flick to take it, barely raising his voice. Flick took the stone and turned it over in her hands.

»*This is for you, overgrounder Flick. With this, you can learn to hear us in your mind.*»

Morris was impressed. Flick never flinched as Njortin spoke into her mind, but her eyes opened wider and her mouthed gaped. »*You stayed with Straag when others would have left him to die. Thank you. Morris has his talisman and this is yours. Speak only in your mind and it will summon us in an emergency. Use it wisely. You are both honorary dragonfriends now. We trust you to hold the secrets of our two layrs safe.*»

There was a deafening roar as all the dragons reacted. Morris understood why Scordril had said 'headpain'. His brain hurt with the noise.

»*Come now and meet the rest of the mages and sit with us. We have others to honour.*» Njortin said. The rest of the dragons seemed to relax, moving, stretching their wings and taking up places on the floor or ledges around the walls. Njortin turned to speak with Scordril.

As Morris and Flick were beckoned to one side by the dragon standing alongside Njortin, a familiar furry face appeared behind the group of mages and AT strutted through, tail in the air, towards the children.

Flick exchanged a glance with Morris. 'How does he seem to know everyone? He looks totally at home,' she said.

Morris shrugged. Their guiding dragon bent slowly to greet the cat.

»*Does AT, I mean Straag, live here? He seems so at home,*» Morris clearly heard Flick ask the dragon. Trust Flick, he thought, to take to mindspeech so easily. The thought was echoed by the green-grey dragon, whom Morris sensed was a female.

»*You mindspeak well, youngone. I am Thofirin, mage of Traprain, dragonmate to Njortin. Straag is indeed at home. He was found half-drowned beside the river as a youngone and rescued by Skolfari and Gullfi, who brought him back to us. He was nursed and raised with our youngones in the layr. He lives with us when he chooses and knows every inch of this layr.*»

Morris stared at the remarkable cat. 'No wonder he's so fierce,' he said to Flick and she laughed as she stroked the strange cat.

A dragon fetched them small slices of roast meat stuffed with something that looked like mashed fruit. Moving slowly amongst the dragons, chewing on their food when they could, they were introduced to so many different ones that Morris felt his head swim with the strange names. Scordril brought over a sleek, blue-grey female dragon with the friendliest golden eyes to meet them, and introduced her as Threah. She welcomed them in a soft and calm voice. Then he and Flick were passed on to Kvayn, the dragonmaster of Musselburgh, with her sad, grey face, who introduced more of the Musselburgh mages. Fenror and Ygdrann were eager to talk to Morris because he, too, came from Musselburgh.

The hall began to smell ever more strongly of dragons, and Morris was beginning to feel he had known dragons all his life. But they were interrupted by a blast of sound like a deep musical note. A hush fell on the dragons. Njortin raised his wings and turned to the rest. A dragon, who Morris recognised as Jarl, came and stood to one side of Scordril in front of Njortin, who called for silence again.

»*This is a day for sadness and for gratitude. And I thank Jarl, now, for helping Straag when he needed it, for caring for the overgrounder girl, but most of all for his bravery in rescuing Yorheim, his kin. In the midst of a battle where we lost Braugnir, Minikk and Kyrekk, who we have remembered this glowbreak, we would have lost more. His bravery will be recorded in the Chronicles, here and in Musselburgh. Step forward, Jarl!*»* Again the dragons roared, some slapping their tails on the ground.

Morris had the urge to put his fingers in his ears, but knew it was pointless. Jarl looked around, and moved only when Scordril pushed him.

Fenror thrust his stubby claws in the air to silence the cheers. »*I, too, declare here that I am a friend of Jarl, Jarl the fearless, Jarl the brave. I was wrong to judge before I knew of the facts.*» Fenror dipped his snout towards Jarl. Other dragon mages rose and joined him. The cheers broke out again.

193

Confused, Morris looked around sensing only that this was as important as the words from Njortin. Then he caught a snippet of conversation between Jarl and the dragon beside him.

»...*I am honoured to have such a younger brother,*» said the strange dragon, very like Jarl for colouring, turning away as if to leave.

»*Thank you, Sygnadi. Your praise is welcome indeed,*» Morris heard Jarl say as he followed behind, and he watched as the two brothers walked away, sensing their conversation but not hearing the words above the noise.

Turning back to the presentations, Morris watched instead as Yorheim, himself, was called out and limped forward in his bandages, assisted by two female dragons. Then Njortin announced that Threah and Ennasif of Musselburgh, who had helped to heal many of the injured during the battle, were to stay for a while and learn more of the Traprain skills. Morris recognised Threah. The other dragon, Ennasif, who was supporting Yorheim, nodded as Yorheim gripped her arm and they stared into each other's eyes.

»*I'm glad you're staying, Ennasif,*» Morris heard Yorheim say.

He noticed Threah smile and step back to join Scordril. Flick nudged Morris.

'Dragons are great,' she yelled into Morris's ear. He nodded. They were certainly brave. But he and Flick had been brave, too. He felt his chest swell with pride. The last day of our holiday, and what a holiday, he thought. Trying to will the time to stop, he reached out and gripped Flick's arm. She nodded, seeming to understand just how important this day was.

'We can never tell anyone, can we?' she asked, her eyes shining. He shook his head. 'Do you think we'll ever meet dragons again?'

'Course we will,' said Morris, and added, 'They gave us the talismans, didn't they!'

'I suppose so,' said Flick, sounding uncertain. Then, holding up her talisman, and twirling it to reflect the light from the fire, she grinned. 'Pity we can't use these to talk to each other about our homework!'

Dragon Dictionary of Useful Words and Phrases

Dragontongue	Meaning	Human Example
Claw-to-claw	Dragon combat without magic or fire	*Hand-to-hand combat*
Dragonbreath	A spell-activating breath, used to open hidden doors, for example	*Using a password to open something*
Dragonclan	Old-fashioned term for dragonkin	*Tribe*
Dragoncloud	Another word for a magecloud	*See magecloud*
Dragondream	Expression used to describe hazy weather, or indistinct thoughts	*Misty weather, or daydream*
Dragonfire	Fire that dragons breath out	*Think blowtorch!*
Dragongrid	A very powerful dragonspell that traps any dragons inside it and makes them powerless to escape	*Think locking the door and throwing away the key!*
Dragonkin	Modern word for an extended dragon family, often widened to cover all dragons past and present.	*Relatives, or tribe*
Dragonmagic	Magic only dragons can do	*Much better than human magician can do!*
Dragonmaster	The leader of the dragons within a single layr and head of the Mage council	*A chairman and mentor*
Dragonmate	Life partner of a dragon	*Partner, wife, husband*
Dragonspan	A measure of distance based on dragon double wingspan	*Old-fashioned term like 'hand-span'*

Dragonsight	Ability to see long distances	*Long range lens or binoculars*
Dragonsnort	Sound made when dragons are irritated	*Disgust*
Dragonclaws!	Used as an oath, rather than a reference to their claws	*Now would we print one here?*
Firetoy	Explosive toys used with a bonfire	*Firework*
Glow/ glow-mark	Day/hour	*Daytime/hour*
Glowbreak	Daybreak	*Sunrise*
Grown	An adult dragon, who has had their layring	*Adult*
Hatchling	Newly hatched dragon	*Baby*
Headpain	Painful interference inside the mind, occurring if mindspeech is too loud	*A splitting headache*
In a million sun-rounds	An expression of impossibility or disbelief	*Never in a million years!*
Layr	Underground home of dragons	*Basement home*
Layring	Coming of age ceremony where a youngone becomes a grown	*Our own coming-of-age birthday celebration*
Link	Mentally connect to another mind	*Use telepathy*
Lying-stone	Long flat stone used by dragons when receiving medical help	*Hospital bed*
Lun	A lunar or moon month, 13 in a sun-round	*Month*

Lunar orb	The moon	Moon
Overgrounder(s)	Human(s)	Us!
Overground	Above ground	Terrestrial
Mage	Senior dragon with magical powers	Wizard, for example
Magecloud	Cloud produced by mage magic, used by flying dragons to hide themselves	Illusion, a smoke screen
Magecouncil	The group of dragons with responsibility for protecting and making decisions on behalf of the layr	Committee or council
Magepower	The special powers only a mage has, such as magesight	Committee or council
Magesight	The extra long-range vision of a mage, usually accompanied by extra sharp senses	Think binoculars or spy camera
Mindlink	Mind-to-mind connection, dragon(s) to dragon(s), or dragon(s) to human(s), to use mindspeech	Telepathic link
Mindspeech	Way of talking mind-to-mind without the use of spoken words	Telepathy
Morph	To change appearance to an overgrounder, or change size as desired	None known
Nightdragon	Dark/black dragons from north	None known, phew!
Not one single dragonseye of remorse	An expression used to mean absolutely no regret	Hard cheese!
Send	Way of mentally sharing images, feelings or thoughts, usually within mindspeech conversation	Think podcast!

Smallone	Very young dragon	Pre-school child
Sun-round	A year	One orbit of the sun, a year
Youngone	Young dragon who has not had their layring yet	Child
Watchdragon	A dragon on watch duties, acting as a lookout	Sentry or guard
Wing	Small formation of flying dragons, normally V-shaped in flight	Think fighter aircraft squadron
Wingrider(s)	Nightdragon rider(s), normally two per dragon, one on each wing, a pilot & a warrior	None known, but you never really know, do you?

Dragon months

Lun-en
Lun-to
Lun-tri
Lun-kvar
Lun-fem
Lun-seks
Lun-shu
Lun-ok
Lun-nau
Lun-dek
Lun-dek-en
Lun-dek-to
Lun-dek-tri

Visit www.lothiandragons.co.uk to read more about Scordril and his world, how the story came to be written and what happened next. You can also find out more about Kelsey Drake.

.

Printed in the United Kingdom
by Lightning Source UK Ltd.
134967UK00001B/355-402/P